T0077940

U SPOILED IT

JOLI

authorHOUSE®

AuthorHouse™
1663 Liberty Drive
Bloomington, IN 47403
www.authorhouse.com
Phone: 833-262-8899

Published by AuthorHouse 12/15/2020

ISBN: 978-1-7283-7258-7 (sc)
ISBN: 978-1-7283-7257-0 (e)

Library of Congress Control Number: 2020916739

Print information available on the last page.

Acknowledgements

First and foremost, I give thanks to God for allowing me to continue with my dream of writing. Writing has always been a passion of mine and something that brings me peace and tranquility. I visualize the characters and get so caught up sometimes that I actually feel as if I know each character.

I would like to thank my children who are the most precious gift I have ever received. The patience and understanding that you have shown throughout my writing process is second to none. I love being your mom and the close bond we have. We are a good team. I love you beyond life. You are the best. There is nothing like the love of family and friends.

My good friend Kenny L. Hardin. You have been a brother to me. You took the time to proofread this novel, laugh at some of the characters, scream at some of the characters and then criticize other characters. You are my sidekick, my confidant, my ride or die and my brother from another mother. I love and appreciate you more than words can express.

Last but never least, I thank you, my readers. I appreciate you riding along with me on this erotic journey. Your support is what makes this worthwhile. It is my desire to bring you a novel that is exciting and one that will entice you to turn the page in anticipation of what will happen next.

U Spoiled It is the sequel to *Don't Spoil It*. It is highly recommended that you read *Don't Spoil It* before reading this novel. Again, my thanks to all of you for the support you have shown me. Much gratitude.

Joli

Chapter 1

At 2:15 a.m. the halls were quiet. The patients were asleep and the only movement was of a few employees shuffling. Lance scurried down the hall quietly. He was supposed to be making his rounds. It was time for him to check his patients and make sure everyone was breathing and had no complications. He unlocked the doors leading into the green zone.

Lance unlocked the door to room #341. Miss Blackwell was asleep with her face turned towards the wall. He tipped past her to her roommate.

"Pssst...pssst! Wake up. Are you ready?"

The patient rubbed her eyes and sat up on the side of the bed. He took her hand and led her to the bathroom. She was very compliant.

Lance recalled the day she was admitted. She walked into the dayroom and stood by the calendar on the wall. Her dark chocolate skin was smooth. Her thickness and the way she swayed her hips when she walked made him stand at attention. There was something different about her and Lance wanted to know what her story was. She seemed like a fish out of water. Her demeanor and the way she carried herself was one of a totally sane woman, yet she was locked away in a mental institution with women who had lost touch with reality.

When Lance introduced himself and explained to her that he would be working on her ward, she flashed him the most beautiful smile he had ever seen. After extending her hand to him and introducing herself, she told him that a misunderstanding had occurred and she was there for an evaluation.

Although he knew her story to be fabricated, he couldn't help but to be attracted to the confident black woman who stood before him. The following night, he pulled a double shift. While on third shift, he came into her room to do a patient check. Lance had not expected her to be awake when he entered her room but as soon as he walked over to her bed, she sat up.

"Can't sleep?" He asked.

"No! I'm hungry." She answered.

"The kitchen is closed. Maybe I can find you a pack of crackers or something to snack on." He responded.

"It's okay." She grabbed his crotch. "This will do just fine."

Lance did not resist when she unzipped his pants and pulled out his manhood. It had come to life with her touch. When she took him in and out of her hot mouth, he grabbed her head. Third shift was a wonderful shift to work over on and he must do it more often. What was it about the muscles in her mouth? It had not been five minutes and he was about ready to explode. Lance prayed that her roommate would not wake up but there was no way in hell that he was going to stop her.

"Mmm…Damn!" He tried not to be loud. "Yes. Ugh!" He held her head tighter, "I'm cummming… Ughhhh!" Lance tried to pull out so he wouldn't put all of that in her mouth. He'd shoot it in his hand. She grabbed the base of his manhood tighter as he moaned and she drained his fluids in her mouth.

"Ahh!" He whispered. "Damn, that felt good. Thanks Nikki."

Nikki licked her lips. "Can a crazy woman make you feel like I just made you feel? That was nothing. I can do so much more."

"I need to make my rounds. Thanks again." Lance zipped his pants up and hurried out of the room. He locked the door and continued to check on his patients. Nikki had made him feel better than his wife ever made him feel. Her mouth was amazing.

After that night, he and Nikki started kicking it on the regular. They could sneak in a session while he worked third shift but soon he went to third shift permanently. Lance was beginning to think there was actually nothing wrong with Nikki. Whenever anyone was around she knew how to be discreet. She never let on that she had any interest or involvement with him.

Now she was in the bathroom bent over, letting him take her in the ass. She had spoiled the hell out of him. It felt good to stick his manhood into her tightness. She took it like a pro. Nikki welcomed his stiff rod. He held her tight around the waist as he stroked long and deep.

"Harder." Nikki whispered. "What are you scared of? Give it to me."

Lance held her tighter as he stroked harder. "Augh! Augh! Nikki!" He couldn't hold back. He pulled his rod out of Nikki and shot cum all over her back. Then Lance beat the head of his rod on her back and finished draining his fluids.

Nikki turned around and kissed him. "Baby it's been a few years now. I'm ready to get out of here. You promised that you would help me. You know for yourself that I don't deserve to be in this place. Am I out of touch with reality? Do I talk to walls? Do I sit in a corner talking to myself?"

Lance shook his head. "No Nikki. You don't do any of that but you're taking your meds on the regular. I just need a little more time. I'm going to have to find you a place somewhere that nobody will think to look. Just be patient. I'll get you out of here. These things take time Sweetheart. This is not something I can just jump up and do overnight. This has to be carefully planned or it won't work." Lance kissed her before locking her in for the night. Nikki made him feel good. Everything he was missing at home, he had found in Nikki. He knew that he was taking a chance by dealing with her. If he ever got caught that would be the end of his career, his marriage and possibly his freedom.

He wondered if she would continue to service him after she got out. There was a possibility she would forget about him. She might return to her kids and her previous life.

Lance wondered why Nikki never talked about her kids. She had given birth to a son while she was there. The staff had whispered about how she showed little or no emotions when the baby was taken from her. He wondered if it were too painful for her to talk about.

One thing for sure, Nikki had her mind set on escaping. He knew from everything he had read in her file that Nikki was not a woman he could cross. He had to find a way to make that happen. Although Nikki made him feel good, he knew there was another side to her.

Chapter 2

Dean ran into the house with the mail. She was a bright child and had adjusted well to her living conditions. It had been almost three years since she was taken from her mother and placed in the home with her dad and stepmother.

Rhonda had accepted Dean and treated her as if she were her own child. She never blamed the child who was the product of her husbands' infidelity. They often had "girls' day out" when they would go play putt-putt, or go shopping and then to McDonalds for a Happy Meal.

Rhonda had barely gotten adjusted to her new lifestyle of motherhood, when she was slapped in the face with a devastating blow. The call came on a cold rainy day. Rhonda had fixed a big pot of chili beans, cole slaw, and pan of cornbread. She had just placed the cornbread on the table when the telephone rang.

"I'll get it." She told her husband Bernard. After a moment Rhonda dropped the telephone and stumbled backwards mumbling, "No! Hell no!"

Her husband pushed his chair back from the table and hurried to get the telephone. He wanted to know who was on the telephone and more importantly what had been said to upset his wife. From her reaction, perhaps someone had died.

"Hello. Who is this? I'm Bernard Simpson. What did you say to my wife? Oh my goodness. This can't be happening. I'll have to call you back." He hung up the telephone and put his arms around Rhonda who had slid to the floor.

"What's wrong Mama? I'm ready for my chili beans." She didn't understand that something was seriously wrong. She was the typical four-year-old child.

"Nothing Baby. Mama is not feeling well. I'm going to fix you a nice big bowl of chili beans and then I am going to lay down. Daddy will eat with you." She managed to say. "But-" Bernard started to object when Rhonda stopped him.

"Later Bernard." She fixed Deans food before going upstairs to her bedroom. Once she was in the bedroom she closed the door and fell back on the bed. Tears filled her eyes. Who the hell did he think she was? Superwoman or something? She was raising one child who was the product of his whoring around. Now the bitch was about to have another child.

Rhonda thought she had put that slut out of her mind but the telephone call and hearing that Nikki was about to give birth to a second child from her husband, brought it all back.

Why had he put his magic stick in her without a cover on it? She wondered when Nikki had gotten pregnant. Did it happen during that first threesome she had let Bernard talk her into? She would never forget how he yelled like a scalded dog when he shot his sperm up in Nikki.

It could have happened on that dreadful day when Nikki held them hostage at gunpoint. She had made them undress and sexed both of them. She sat on Bernard and rode him like she was on a wild bull in a rodeo. Rhonda wondered after it was all over, how her husband had managed such a hard magic stick under such a stressful situation. When Nikki slid her wet pussy down on his magic stick, Rhonda had noticed how he stiffened his legs. He acted like he wanted his magic stick there in her pussy.

After dinner, Bernard fixed Dean's bath water and joined Rhonda in the bedroom.

"Baby, I'm sorry," He told her. "I don't know what else to say. I prayed that Nikki wouldn't be pregnant. You know this is not what I wanted."

"Yeah, but you wanted the pussy didn't you?" Rhonda was hurt. "You didn't even try to reason with her. You sat in that chair with your hard ass magic stick while she bounced on it and you didn't try to reason with her."

"Come on now baby. That's not fair. When in the hell has anyone ever been able to reason with Nikki?"

"Rhonda kept recalling that day. Even though Bernard's hands were tied behind his back, he had no problem getting his dick hard so Nikki could slide it into her wetness. As much as he had tried to hide it, his facial expression was acknowledgement that he enjoyed it. She silently prayed that Nikki would get off him before he shot off but the moans that escaped his mouth and the look of pleasure on Nikki's face let her know. Nikki had gotten what she wanted. Bernard's sperm.

"Rhonda, all I can do is apologize and I have done that so many times. We are back on track now and Nikki wants nothing better than to destroy that. If you allow her to destroy us, she will. We have come too far and dealt with too much to let Nikki come in and ruin it." Bernard was pleading his case but Rhonda had to get it off her chest.

"So what am I suppose to say? Am I supposed to act like it is great news? Am I supposed to rejoice at the thought of having a new addition to the family? Is that what the hell I am supposed to do? Are you crazy? I can't keep doing this!" She cried. "I just can't."

"And I'm not asking you to." Bernard told her. "I could never ask you to take another child. Honey, you know that I could never put you through that humiliation. They will just have to find placement for him Rhonda."

She hated him all over again. Bernard had turned her world upside down with his whoring. The minute he decided to put his magic stick in another woman, he changed the coarse of their marriage. If it were not bad enough that he was unfaithful, he had chosen a woman who was mentally unstable. With her giving birth to his children, there was no mistake that he would be forever connected to her.

Rhonda knew she could not separate the children. It wouldn't be fair to Dean to have her brother raised by foster parents. And what about Bernard? Even though he swore he would understand if she didn't take the child, how could she be sure? Nikki was about to give him a son. All men dreamt of having a son, didn't they? Eventually he might grow to resent her. Isn't that what the hell men did? Didn't they have a habit of shifting the blame? Even though he had caused the problem, he would find a way to blame Rhonda for him not having his son with him, or worse; his son might grow up to hate him. She didn't see where she had much of a choice.

Nikki named the baby Bernard Simpson Jr. Rhonda nicknamed him Nard. Dean was excited to have her brother living with them. She helped change his diapers, bathe him and feed him.

That seemed like a lifetime ago. Dean was now six years old and Nard was in his terrible two's. Rhonda took the mail from Dean before tickling her stomach. Dean laughed and then ran into the den where Nard was on the floor playing with sticks. She went through each piece of mail, tossing the junk mail aside. Water bill, credit card statement, cell phone, and *WHAT?* Rhonda gasped as she fixed her eyes on an envelope from Brooksville Mental Institution.

It was addressed to her but she wasn't sure why. Nikki was not supposed to have any contact with the Simpson's or the kids. As soon as she opened the envelope, Rhonda recognized Nikki's very neat handwriting. At a glance, no one would suspect the letter to have been written by someone of Nikki's mentality.

She read: *Sshh…Baby! This is our lil secret. Mama misses eating that moist cookie. It's been a while and I can't stop thinking about you. You have been in my dreams lately. I hope you are saving that cookie for me. Please don't make the mistake of letting anybody spoil it. I couldn't stand the thought of anybody else having what is mine. Keep that cookie tight for me Baby. It won't be long and Mama will be feasting on that sweet cookie. If anybody has touched it, I will be able to tell and I am going to take a dagger and crumble that cookie up. Do you understand? Ha…ha…ha! I'm just kidding. You know I wouldn't harm my cookie. I love you.*

Nikki Boo

Rhonda crumbled the letter up and held it in her hand. Why was Nikki writing her again after all this time? And why was she claiming that they'd be seeing each other soon. Had she lost track of time? Didn't she understand that she had been sentenced to seven years in a mental institution with no possibility for early release? Rhonda got up with the crumbled letter and threw it in the trash. Nikki was not going to cause problems for her.

She couldn't help but to remember how good Nikki made her feel. The bitch was crazy as hell but there was something about the way she made love to Rhonda that was very satisfying. No one had ever made her juices flow like Nikki had. Rhonda shook her head. She didn't want to think about it. That was a crazy time in her life. Although Nikki had made her feel good, she was half scared of that bitch. Nikki was capable of just about anything. Rhonda rubbed her hand across the side of her face as her mind drifted back to that first time Nikki slapped her. Yeah!

That bitch was in the right place. A mental institution was exactly where she needed to be.

Rhonda wondered if she should mention the letter to Bernard. He had not mentioned Nikki's name since they went to Brooksville to pick Nard up. Nikki had wanted his nickname to be Junior but Rhonda couldn't stand the thought of calling him Junior. When she suggested they call him Nard, her husband agreed.

After thinking about it for a while, she decided not to tell Bernard about the letter. She retrieved the crumbled letter and tore it into tiny pieces before flushing it.

Chapter 3

Nikki looked at the clock. It was 12:15 a.m. and Lance was scheduled to be off. That meant Karen would be in. She was the part-time nurse who filled in on the nights Lance was off.

Good! Nikki thought. *I don't have to be bothered with his stupid ass tonight. He makes me sick and I am tired of being bothered with his no fucking ass. If he doesn't hurry up and get me the hell out of here he will be sorry. I mean that shit! I'm not playing with his motherfuckin ass.*

She walked over to check on her roommate. The bitch snored like she had sleep apnea but she was the perfect roommate. When she was awake she spent her days looking out the window and chewing her tongue. Nikki once thought she was chewing gum. *"Stop chewing that fuckin gum like that Bitch."* She recalled telling her. But the woman kept chewing. *"Spit that shit out. No wonder you are in here. You are chewing that damn gum like it is your last meal."* When Nikki's roommate spit nothing out, Nikki had walked over to her and forced her mouth open. Mildred didn't have anything in her mouth or under her tongue. When she closed her mouth again, she continued chewing, only harder. It didn't take Nikki long to figure out that she was chewing her tongue, or imaginary gum or something. She decided she would just ignore Mildred. The bitch obviously had problems.

After glancing at her roommate, Nikki stood by the door. She heard the keys turn in the door before it opened. As soon as the nurse walked in and closed the door, Nikki approached her. "I've missed you Babe. You need to be here more than part-time." The nurse stood with her back to the door while Nikki kissed her.

Karen was glad that she only worked part-time. Nikki was crazy and she regretted ever getting involved with her. She felt like a trapped animal. There was no way she could get rid of Nikki without getting herself in trouble. When she initially got involved with Nikki, she was very vulnerable. She had been dating a doctor for eight months and was in love with him. When her shift ended early one night, she went to Erik's house to surprise him. Upon walking onto the porch of his dimly lit house she heard quiet moans coming from his bedroom. Instead of ringing the doorbell, she had squeezed behind the hedges and looked through the sheer window curtains. She could see Erik on the bed being held up by his hands and knees while his P.A. stroked him deep in his ass. Karen had run blindly through the hedges scratching her arms and face as she tried to escape the scene that had just played before her eyes. She was devastated.

The next night when she covered Lance's shift, Nikki was awake and, in the bathroom, when Karen unlocked the doors. She noticed the scratches on Karen's face and asked her what was wrong. Karen didn't want to talk about it. Nikki brushed her hands across Karen's face and kissed the scratches. Tears rolled down Karen's cheeks.

"It'll be okay. Who did this to you? He doesn't deserve you." Nikki looked at Karen and waited for an answer.

"No one. I scratched myself in some hedges." She answered Nikki.

"Then why are you upset? I can tell that you are hurt. Go ahead. I'm a good listener." Nikki tried to coax Karen into telling her what was wrong.

"It's nothing. I've got to go finish my rounds." Karen turned to walk away. Nikki stopped her.

"Your face is all wet. You don't want to go out there looking like that do you?" She wiped Karen's face before kissing her on the lips. "Let me make it better." She moved her mouth to Karen's neck and started sucking on her neck. It was as if she knew it was a hot spot for Karen. The nurse stood there and leaned her head back. She relaxed while Nikki sucked her neck and made her feel good. Nikki stuck her hands in Karen's pants. Karen tried to stop her.

"Nah! Just calm down and relax. Please. Let me feel your sweet fruit. I know it's sweet."

Karen had never been with a woman before. She had never entertained the thought of another woman touching her. But she wanted to be touched and she stood there slightly opening her legs while Nikki inserted her fingers into her wetness. It either felt good or she was lonelier than she realized. She didn't know which. She only knew that in a matter of minutes she was cumming while Nikki was fingering her and tongue kissing her. Erik had never made her feel like that.

Afterwards, she used a hand towel from Nikki's bathroom to clean up. She didn't know what to say to Nikki. It had felt good but Karen knew that she never should have let a patient touch her inappropriately like that. What the hell was she thinking about?

"I have to go." She told Nikki. She quickly walked out of the room making sure the door was locked behind her.

The next week when she came to work, she didn't want to face Nikki. She felt guilty and hoped that Nikki had forgotten all about that night. She doubted it though because Nikki was somehow different from most of the other patients. She seemed to be more in touch with reality. Karen unlocked the door hoping Nikki was sleep but as luck would have it, she was wide-awake.

"Come on in. Mama's been waiting on you." Nikki sat up in bed. "Are you going to let me taste that sweet fruit tonight? I tasted your juices off my fingers and I couldn't get enough of you. I need to have my tongue in you."

Karen was stunned. "No Nikki. I'm sorry. That never should have happened last week. I was just going through something and I wasn't thinking clearly. We could both get in trouble for that. I apologize."

"There is no need to apologize." Nikki moved towards her. "I won't spoil it. As long as you don't spoil it nobody has to know. But I can't end things without putting my mouth on my fruit. You're as sweet as a Georgia peach."

Karen didn't understand what Nikki meant by the comment, *my fruit*. What the hell?

"Hurry up!" Nikki told her. "If you don't want anybody to find out what happened between us, take off your pants."

I can't do that." Karen protested. "Please. I was vulnerable. I had just caught my man with his fuckin lover. I'm sorry. Please don't make me do this." She knew that she had made the biggest mistake of her life getting involved with Nikki and her hands were tied.

Nikki was serious. "Please don't make you do WHAT? I'm not making you do shit. I'm asking you as nicely as I fuckin can to take off those damn pants and lay your damn Latino ass down on the bed so Mama can taste her sweet fruit." Nikki's voice had suddenly turned harsh and satanic.

Karen had messed up. If this one time would satisfy Nikki and keep the crazo off her back, she'd do it. She slipped out of her pants in the dark and lay on Nikki's bed. If the crazy ass woman wanted to eat her fruit, she'd let her eat it, fake an orgasm, and finish her rounds.

Nikki spread Karen's legs and fell to her knees. She licked around Karen's clit slowly before inserting her fingers into Karen's wetness.

This can't be happening. Oh my goodness. This feels good. Damn! I can't take it. Karen thought. "YEEEES!" She said out loud surprising herself. "Oh damn! You're making me feel good." She couldn't help it. Nikki was eating the hell out of her fruit. She hadn't intended on cumming for Nikki but electricity ran through every vein in her body as Nikki devoured her fruit. Suddenly Nikki stopped.

Karen grabbed her head. "No. Please don't stop. I'm almost there."

"Whose fruit is this?' Nikki asked.

"Don't stop!" Karen ignored her. "Please don't stop. I need to finish this. Let me cum." She begged.

"Maybe you didn't hear me." Nikki slowly fingered Karen, teasing her. "Whose fruit is this?" She asked again.

"Yours! It's your fruit." She answered, desperate to cum.

"That's what I know, and I take care of mine." Nikki continued to eat Karen's fruit until she brought her to a climax. Karen trembled uncontrollably as Nikki pleased her.

"Ah…oh yesssssss." She moaned. She tried to push Nikki's head away but she refused to stop until she had completely drained Karen. Afterwards, the nurse barely had enough strength to stand.

After that night, Nikki would not leave her alone. She claimed the fruit as her own. Karen enjoyed her but hated that Nikki was so controlling. She told Nikki she wanted out.

"There is no getting out until I'm ready to get out. While Mama is in here you are my bitch. If you want out, find you another damn job. But as long as you are here, make sure you keep my fruit juicy for me." Nikki looked her straight in the eyes without blinking.

"Give Mama a kiss to seal the deal." Karen kissed Nikki and walked out of the room.

Now Karen dreaded having to tell Nikki she was moving to first shift. She didn't know how Nikki would take it but she knew that she had to do something to escape the clutches of the crazed lunatic. First shift was the only alternative she could come up with. After Nikki kissed her, she looked at the floor.

"Nikki, we are not going to be able to see each other at night any more. They are moving me to first shift. When I come in next week I will be on mornings. That's going to cut out our alone time." She was nervous not knowing what kind of reaction to expect from Nikki. The last thing in the world she needed was for Nikki to become unglued and get her in trouble. Not only could she be fired but she could also be brought up on charges for molesting a mental patient. That would have been an injustice in her opinion because Nikki seemed saner than half of the staff at Brooksville.

Nikki took a few steps backward. "How the hell did that happen Baby? Why are they fuckin with us like this?"

"I don't know." Karen lied. "They needed someone else on first shift and I was the only part-time person working third shift. Besides that, I have less seniority. I'm going to miss you."

Karen watched while Nikki fell back on the bed. "If this is the way it's going to be, you need to give Mama something to remember you by. Get your ass down here and eat Mama."

Nikki spread her legs and parted the lips of her pussy in the dimly lit room. Karen knelt down in front of her. The dimness of the room could not hide the big, black, curly hairs that covered Nikki's pussy. Karen wondered how she had allowed Nikki to turn her out. Nikki was a pretty dark-skinned woman who weighed well over two hundred pounds. Her thighs were thick and she was blessed with a phatt ass. Karen licked Nikki's clit, which was so hard, and big it could have easily been mistaken for anything other than a clitoris. As she started pleasing her, Nikki's hands moved to her hair.

"Oh yeah Baby. Eat Mama. Ah! Make me feel good. Make this a night for me to remember Baby."

Karen suddenly stopped and jumped to her feet.

"What the fuck is wrong with you Bitch? I didn't cum. And I didn't tell your ass to stop." Nikki sat up and awaited a response.

"I thought I heard someone in the hall." Karen told her. "I need to finish my rounds. I will be back soon. Let me check things out." She moved towards the door.

Nikki sprang from the bed and hurried to the door. She swung Karen around and put her hand in Karen's pants, while backing her up against the wall. She put two fingers in Karen's fruit and moved them in and out, hard and fierce.

"You're hurting me." Karen protested.

"Shut the fuck up. Why is my fruit so damn dry?" Nikki pressed her body hard against Karen. She stuck her tongue in Karen's mouth. After they kissed she moved her mouth to the nurse's ear and stuck her tongue in. "We're going to try this shit again. You're going to eat Mama and you are not going to stop until I cum. Do you understand?"

"Yes!" Karen answered. She was glad this was her last night. Nikki was crazy as hell when she wanted to be. "I understand. I want to please you Mama. It's just that I thought I heard keys down the hall."

She followed Nikki to the bed. The lunatic was ready to be pleased. She lay there naked with her knees bent and legs spread apart.

Karen knelt on the floor again and was within tongue's reach of Nikki when keys turned in the door and it swung open. She froze. What could she say? There was no way to get out of it. She was on the floor with her head between the legs of a mental patient.

"Excuse me. I'm sorry. I will come back later. I didn't mean to interrupt." Lance told the women as he slowly began to pull the door closed.

Karen jumped up. "Lance please! I know this doesn't look good. I …don't want to lose my…job."

"Lance! Don't you dare close that damn door. Get your ass over here and show this bitch how Mama likes to be taken care of." Nikki demanded.

Karen was shocked to say the least. Was Nikki doing the entire staff? Damn! "I'll be back. I've been gone too long." Karen told the two.

"Splash your face and be back here in ten damn minutes or else. When you get back we are going to have some fun. Lance is going to fuck both of us tonight."

"What about Mildred?" Karen asked. "She could wake up at any time."

Nikki, who was facing Lance, suddenly swung around with a backhand that rested across Karen's face. "Bitch, don't you ever question me about anything. Do you understand me? I will whup your damn ass until you can't see straight. Now hurry up so you can get back to Mama."

When Karen left, Nikki turned her attention back to Lance. "Are you ready to freak?"

He grabbed the crotch of his pants. "Hell yeah."

Chapter 4

Brandi barely knew which day of the week it was as she stumbled onto the porch. After being unable to find her keys, she rang the doorbell. A sleepy and tired Shemeka opened the door. She helped Brandi to the couch.

The two had been roommates for a few years. Shemeka had originally intended to stay only long enough to sell her house and get her head together. After she witnessed the death of her lover at the hands of his cousin Nikki in her living room, she could no longer stay there.

Things worked out well. They shared the expenses as they both tried to cope with losing the one they loved. Shemeka had become devastated upon finding out that her lover Robert was actually a woman whose birth name was Roberta. She had fallen in love before she realized the truth.

Brandi had lost her boyfriend Anthony. He was in the Federal Penitentiary and she hadn't stuck by him thinking she could no longer deal with the prison system. When she realized Anthony was whom she wanted to be with, he had gotten an early release and moved on with his ex-girlfriend Jessica.

Brandi was a pretty white woman with a black woman's ass. She had only dated a few guys since Anthony and none of them seemed to satisfy the void left by Anthony. She seemed to spend her spare time in bars. Shemeka feared that her friend would become and alcoholic.

"You're going to have to stop this drinking Brandi. What if you would have had an accident? You could have killed somebody. You could have killed yourself." Shemeka fluffed the pillows on the couch behind Brandi's back.

"No! Just talk to me." She patted the couch with her hand. "Sit right here." Brandi's speech was slurred. "What's wrong with me Meka? I try and I try but nothing works out. I'm not happy and I am never going to be happy. Not as long as Anthony is with Jessica." She cried.

"Girl, you have to get over that. It's been about three years. What are you going to do? Drink yourself to death?" Shemeka was sleepy. She wanted to go back to bed. Why the hell was Brandi having a pity party at 2:30 a.m.? "Let's get some rest and we will talk about it in the morning."

"I saw them!" She shouted. "They didn't see me but I saw them. They were at a table in the corner. He was kissing all over her like she was something good to eat. It should have been me with him."

Shemeka didn't want to stay up the rest of the morning talking about Anthony. He had moved on. If she really loved him she would want him to be happy. She had her chance.

Anthony had done well after his release. He had gone to truck driving school and landed a job with a trucking company. From everything she had heard, he was thriving and on the right track since his release.

"Brandi, you're going to have to get yourself together or I don't know what is going to happen. Get some rest. We'll talk in the morning. Come on gal. Let me help you in the shower."

Meka helped Brandi up. She wondered how Brandi was going to be able to function. She undressed Brandi and checked the temperature of the water before helping her into the shower. She washed her friend's hair first and then lathered and washed her body. Brandi offered no assistance with her shower. "Spread your legs girl. You're going to have me soaked." Shemeka told her.

When Brandi was clean and smelling fresh, Meka toweled her dry and helped her into a gown. She pulled back the covers and helped her into bed. "Goodnight Brandi."

Shemeka went to her room and stepped out of her wet pj's before putting on an oversized tee shirt. She closed her eyes and drifted to sleep. In a few hours it would be daylight.

Chapter 5

Karen splashed her face near the nurse's station to make sure she was seen by some of the other employees. Reluctantly she made her way back down the dimly lit hall. *What the hell have I gotten myself into? I'll never be rid of that crazy ass bitch. She could cause me to lose my job. And what the hell is up with her and Lance? How did he let himself get involved with a patient?*

Karen used her key to unlock the door. Nikki was sitting up on the side of the bed waiting. Lance was nowhere in sight. Nikki stood and licked her lips. "It's clear." She said.

Lance emerged from the bathroom. Karen had always thought he was cute. He stood six-feet two inches tall, clean-shaven with a vanilla wafer complexion and sexy hazel eyes. His muscular build showed undeniable signs that he spent many hours in the gym working out. He never had much to say to her and Karen had always thought he was stuck up. Now, he was standing before her, naked from the waist down. His manhood looked to be about seven and a half inches soft, as it hung between his legs.

"Nikki, I don't know. I'm scared. If someone comes in here we are all screwed. And what if Mildred wakes up? It's just too risky. If I lose my job and -"

"Shut the hell up with that damn whining. You haven't been worried about your job so don't start now. Mildred has downed two sleeping pills. Go ahead and undress so we can make this a quickie. Mama's been waiting long enough."

Nikki walked over to Lance and kissed him. She took his hand and led him to the bed where Karen sat. She whispered in his ear. "Let's make sure she enjoys this. It is her last night on third and I want it to be one that she will never forget. We are going to have some fun tonight."

She actually enjoyed Karen more than she did Lance. He was a damn wimp and she only fooled with him for convenience. She knew she could eventually talk him into helping her escape. He was an insecure bastard with a big ass nine-inch tool that he didn't know how to use.

Lance stood next to the bed and watched as Nikki tilted Karen backwards on the bed. Karen was tense and nervous as Nikki spread her legs apart and touched her. "Relax! Mama has everything under control." Nikki whispered before tasting her fruit.

Karen wanted the ordeal to be over quickly. She was not comfortable. She glanced to the right and saw Lance standing there in the darkness stroking his manhood, which grew to about nine inches. *Damn! I bet that really would feel nice up in me.* She began to relax as Nikki sucked the sweetness of her juicy fruit. The moans that eluded from Karen's mouth caused Lance to stroke his manhood harder.

"Hey! Don't forget about me. Don't leave me out of the fun."

Nikki lifted her head and pulled Lance in front of her. She took his manhood in her hand and licked around the head of it before taking him in her mouth. It turned Karen on to watch them. She touched her fruit. She inserted her fingers in her wetness and then she tasted how good her fruit was. Nikki took Lance out of her mouth and tapped Karen on the leg. "Get up."

"What the hell?" Lance questioned as Karen stood. "Are you going to leave me like this?" He looked down at the stiffness he was holding in his hand.

"Shhh! It's time for Mama to be taken care of." Nikki looked past Lance to Karen. "Don't think you are leaving third shift without eating me. We are in this together. Hurry up before someone starts to look for you. Get your ass down here and take care of Mama."

Karen walked to the foot of the bed. She climbed up on the bed and started pleasing Nikki. Lance stood there jacking his meat until Nikki said, "Go ahead. Fuck her in the ass while she is eating Mama."

Without hesitation, Lance hurried to position himself behind Karen. He spread the cheeks of her ass and put the head of his stiff rod on her opening. As he worked the head in, she tensed up and jumped. "Take it easy. Damn!"

"I'm sorry." He said while backing up and pulling out. Lance went over to the dresser where a bottle of lotion was and squeezed some onto his hands. He saturated his rod and tried again while Karen continued to please Nikki.

"Um… this ass is tight" He muttered as he tried to go deeper into Karen.

"No! Stop! You're hurting me." Karen told him as he tried to thrust deeper in her tight ass. "Take it out! That shit hurts."

Nikki grabbed a handful of Karen's hair and yanked her head. "Shut the fuck up Bitch and eat my damn pussy. Hold that ass still and let Lance finish."

"But he's hurting me. I can't do this." Karen spoke in a raised voice.

Lance ignored her cries and pressed on as he gripped her tightly. "Oh damn this ass feels good. Please don't make me stop. Ahh… yeah."

"Fuck her!' Nikki demanded. "Fuck that ass until you cum."

"No!" Karen yelled as she tried to stand. "Stop Lance. I've got to go. They'll be looking for me. Let me up." She pushed back and freed herself.

"Damn Karen! I was almost up in there. What the hell you do that for?" He held his rod in his hand stroking it vigorously. "I need to finish this. Damn!" Suddenly Lance stopped stroking himself and forgot his need to cum.

Nikki had put her hands around Karen's neck and was choking her. Karen was gasping for air. "Bitch don't you ever try to play me again. Do you know whom the hell you are dealing with? Mama won't think twice about breaking your fuckin neck and making it look like an accident. Understand?"

Karen nodded her head to signal that she understood. Tears rolled down her face as she tried to speak. "I …I…uh…I…can't…bre…athe." Nikki pushed her back before releasing her.

Lance watched in silence. Karen bent to gather her clothes. Nikki kicked her. "Don't make it happen Bitch. Next time come correct." She looked at Lance whom was speechless. "Put your clothes on and get the hell out of here. We were about to have some fun until this dumb bitch spoiled it. Never again."

Lance and Karen both quickly dressed. She unlocked the door and checked both sides of the corridor before exiting the room. Lance exited right behind. Karen went to the right and Lance to the left.

Nikki sat in the center of the bed with her knees bent to her chest and her arms wrapped around her legs. *I've got to get the fuck out of here before I snap and hurt that bitch. Lance better not go back on his word. He better get me out of here soon if he knows what is good for him.* She stretched her legs and slid down in bed. *Karen wants to act all damn stupid like she can't take it in the ass. I've got something for her.* Nikki pulled the covers up over her and turned over on her side. *That bitch will move to first shift over my dead damn body. If she doesn't know whom she's messing with, she better ask some damn body.*

Chapter 6

Shemeka and Brandi were already seated when Rhonda arrived at Apple Bees. The three had decided to meet for lunch and have girl talk. Shemeka waved her hand when she saw Rhonda walk into the restaurant.

The waitress approached the table to take their order. Brandi was just finishing up a Bahamas Mama she had ordered at the bar." I'll have another one of these." She told the waitress while holding her glass up.

Shemeka glanced at Rhonda. They had often conversed and expressed concern over Brandi's drinking. They both feared there was a possibility that she would become an alcoholic. For some reason, she couldn't seem to shake the breakup with Anthony.

"Diet sprite for me." Shemeka said.

"Okay." The waitress responded. "I'll put your drink order in while I give you a few minutes to look over the menu." She turned and walked away.

"So what's been up with you gals?" Rhonda asked as she looked over the menu.

"Nothing new." Shemeka answered. "Brandi is still obsessing over Anthony. I'm still trying to get her to move on and I still feel like I am fighting a losing battle."

Brandi interjected. "And I still feel like I am living with my mother,"

"Well listen to this." Rhonda changed the subject. "I got a letter from that crazy ass Nikki."

"What? Are you serious?" Shemeka asked. "Do you mean that bitch had the nerve to write you? I still say that she is not crazy. Her ass is pretending. She should have been given life in prison." Shemeka felt a twinge of pain as she remembered how Nikki tried to kill her and Robert had thrown himself in the path of the bullet. That bullet had taken his life shortly after she had found out that Robert was actually Roberta.

The waitress returned with their drinks. "Are you ready to order of do you need more time?"

"We're ready." Brandi answered. "I'll have the riblet basket. Substitute the fries for baked potato."

"Give me the hot wings with fries." Shemeka added.

"Mild, medium, or hot?" The waitress asked.

"Medium. I can't do the hot. Tried that before and needed a pitcher of water to cool my tongue."

"Okay. Well that leaves me. I think I will have the grilled chicken salad with ranch dressing."

"I'll get your order right in." The waitress walked away.

"Now back to our conversation Rhonda. What the hell did that bitch want? Why did she write you?" Brandi was curious. She knew that Nikki was not playing with a full deck.

"She just wanted to put my nerves on edge. For some reason she thinks she is about to get out and I guess she wants to see the kids." Rhonda didn't want to get into the contents of the letter. Shemeka and Brandi were her girls but she had never shared with them the fact that she had let Bernard talk her into a threesome involving Nikki. She didn't want them to know she had indulged in sexual dealings with the nut case. The woman was a monster and she could almost kick her own ass for even letting Bernard talk her into it.

"Let's not ruin our meal by talking about that crazo." Brandi stood. "Excuse me for a minute. I need to use the lil girl's room."

"Rhonda, I'm really worried about her. She's drinking almost every day. I've found a house but I don't know if I really feel comfortable moving out and leaving her alone."

"Maybe we should intervene and see about getting her some help."

"The only help she wants is Anthony and he has moved on about his business."

The waitress returned with their food. "Is there anything else I can get for you?"

"No." Rhonda answered. "We're fine."

Brandi walked back to the table where her friends were seated. "Good! Our food is here. I'm starving." She turned towards the opposite side of the restaurant where she heard the sound of a man's laughter. A laugh she would recognize anywhere. Her eyes stopped on Anthony as the waitress seated Jessica and him diagonally and three seats from them. He looked happy. Anthony held Jessica's hand above the table and slowly brought it to his lips. He kissed her hand and gently placed it on the table. Brandi couldn't seem to take her eyes off them.

Rhonda and Shemeka turned to see who had captured her attention. "Do you want to leave?" Shemeka asked. "We can get carry out boxes and take our food back to the house."

"No Meka. That's nonsense. We are bound to run into them every now and again. I can't run every time I see them. I'm good." She picked up a riblet and took a bite. Besides, I don't like warmed over baked potatoes."

The waitress refilled the water glass for Rhonda and told Shemeka she'd be right back with her a diet sprite.

"I'll have another Bahamas Mama." Brandi said.

"Sure. Coming right up."

"Brandi, don't you think you have had enough to drink?" Shemeka asked.

"Don't worry Ma. I've got this."

"That's crazy." Rhonda joined in. "You're sitting here gulping down drinks and turning yourself into a drunk. For what? Because you can't have Anthony? Men come and go. Relationships end all the damn time. Get over it."

"You're right." Brandi looked towards Jessica and Anthony. "He's not worth it. I'll be right back." She stood and walked to the table where her ex-boyfriend was seated with the new woman in his life.

"Hi. I saw y'all sitting over here and I just wanted to come over and speak. You look well Anthony. How are things going with you?"

He reached across the table to take Jessica's hand in his. "Cudn't be betta. How bout you?" He was casually dressed and flashed a big Colgate smile. Jessica wore a spaghetti strapped dress and seemed to be overdressed for Apple Bee's. Brandi couldn't help but notice the large diamond that adorned her finger. It must have cost a fortune.

"I'm doing great. Staying busy." Brandi answered. "Well let me get back to my friends. Take care." She needed to get away from the table before she threw up. *How the hell could he give Jessica a ring like that? Bastard. Even though we ended the relationship, I'm the one who rode it out with his black ass during the prison years. Hell. Jessica didn't even bother to visit him. I was the one who took all the fuckin risk and could have gotten locked up for smuggling drugs into the prison. I do all the work and Jessica gets the reward.*

Brandi took her seat at the table. "Yall won't believe this shit!"

"What made you go over there?" Shemeka asked. "What were you expecting?"

"Not to see a rock big enough to blind my ass."

"Damn!" Rhonda was as surprised as Brandi had been. Neither she nor Shemeka had approved of Brandi's relationship with Anthony. "That's like a slap in the face but remember that you're the one who called it off so you can't really complain."

"But I was with him through the worse of it. And I still love him. I just got sidetracked." She was hurt. At one time she had plans of spending the rest of her life with Anthony. Things took a u-turn when she was informed that he would not be getting out as soon as she had thought. "I've suddenly lost my appetite. Please excuse me. I've got to get the hell out of here."

"We'll all leave. Let me flag the waitress and I'll take care of the check." Rhonda offered.

After Rhonda paid for the meals, they all left. She understood Brandi's pain but felt that it was time for her friend to face reality. Reality was that Anthony had moved on with his life without her.

Chapter 7

Lance dressed for work, kissed his wife and headed out the door. When he pulled into the parking lot at Brooksville, he sat in his car for a while. *Twenty minutes before my shift starts. What the hell am I going to tell Nikki? She's expecting me to tell her something tonight and I don't have a damn clue about how I am going to help her escape.* He turned the ignition off and got out of the car. After making his way through the dimly lit halls, he stopped at the employee's lounge to grab a cup of coffee.

I've got to find a way to get her out of here. And soon or there is no telling what she'll do. I love her but there is a side to Nikki that scares the hell out of me.

After a while, Lance reported to duty. The good thing about working third shift was that all the bosses were gone. The big wheels only worked first shift.

"Hello Lance. How are you?" Miss Covington asked. She was a short stubby white woman with gray hair. Everybody knew she was 68 years old and could have retired. However, she always claimed to be 58 years old and looking forward to retirement. The staff played along with her to humor her and to keep from hurting her feelings. It was common knowledge that her daughter was strung out on drugs. Miss

Covington had custody of her four grandchildren, which made it nearly impossible for her to retire.

"Hello Miss Covington. What did you bring good for me to eat tonight? Lance asked.

"Ahh! Young man I brought you a bowl of my famous peach cobbler. I hope you enjoy it." Miss Covington stuck her hand inside the plaid lunch tote and handed Lance a bowl with a lid on it. He could smell the aroma of the cobbler seeping through the lid. She always brought him a treat when they both worked third. "Good ole peach cobbler is good for anything that ails you son. Now you get along to work. I've got things to do."

As Lance watched Miss Covington whisk her way down the hall and out of sight, he wished that he too could vanish. *How much longer before Nikki blanks on my ass? I care about her and she makes me feel good but is she going to be the one to destroy me?*

Lance put the cobbler away and checked the patient's charts. It had been an uneventful day and he prayed that the night would be just as peaceful. He unlocked the doors of the corridor, which housed room #341, and his heart began to beat a little faster. He walked down the corridor, bypassing the other rooms and stopping at Nikki's door.

"Please be sleep." He mumbled. "For goodness sake! Just for tonight. Lord let her be knocked out on some medicine or something."

When Lance opened the door, Nikki was standing in the center of the room. He knew that was not a good sign because she was usually on the bed when he came in. He walked to where she stood and kissed her.

"Lance." She whispered as she touched both sides of his face with her hands. "Do you have some good news for me?"

"Nikki, I'm trying. I promise you that it won't be much longer. I'm working on something. I just have to make sure it's going to work. Trust me."

"Sure! I trust you. And I want you to trust me." She unzipped his pants and pulled out his manhood. Lance stood there while she held him tight in her hand. He waited for her to drop to her knees like she had done so many times in the past. Instead, she left one hand at the base of his pride and joy while she took the other and twisted it like she was wringing out a mop. He gasped.

"Whoa! Damn Nikki. Hold up." He spoke in a loud whisper while trying to free himself from her grasp. The more he tried to free himself, the worse the pain got.

"Do you really know who you are dealing with? I own this motherfucka. It's attached to your body so it's mine. Right? Is it mine?"

Lance nodded. "It's yours." He wanted Nikki to loosen her grip on him. She couldn't possibly know how painful that was. "Please let go Nikki. I love you. I'm goanna work it out."

Nikki released her hold on him and chuckled. "Ah,ha,ha,ha! You are so damn funny Lance. I love you too. I'd never hurt you. I'm sorry. I just got carried away. Being locked up in this place just makes me crazy. You have to get me out of here Boo. Soon. I'm serious Lance. I want to be free so we don't have to sneak like this."

"Nikki, I've thought of something but I'll need Karen's help to pull it off. Do you think she'll get on board?"

"She'll get on board. Just let her know what she has to do." Nikki smiled. "Now lay back and let Mama make you feel good."

Lance was hesitant as he moved closer to the bed. He was scared to do it and scared not to do it. Suppose Nikki decided to take a bite this time? Knowing he was at her mercy, he obeyed and soon relaxed while she took him in and out of her mouth. Within minutes his legs had stiffened and he was doing the jerk.

"Let me clean up and get out of here before someone starts to look for me." Lance wet a washcloth in the restroom and cleaned up. He was scared to trust Nikki. He had to somehow come up with a plan. He would need Karen's help but first he needed a plan. He had bought a little time but Nikki was a smart woman. He wouldn't be able to bluff again. He kissed her before leaving.

Nikki stood in her room looking at her roommate who was sound asleep. Mildred's sleeping pills always guaranteed her a good night sleep. *What if she would wake up one night and catch us? What if that sorry ass Lance doesn't come through for me and I have to make sure Mildred catches us? Or what if I set him up for the administrator to catch us? I can tell them he has been raping me since I got here and I'm scared of him. I can tell them he comes in at night and takes my sweetness. Yeah! That motherfucka don't know. I'll shake his world all to hell. He better hurry up and get me the fuck outta here.*

Chapter 8

Brandi was curled up on the couch when her phone rang. She glanced at it and turned back over on the couch. She very seldom answered calls from people who refused to let their number be shown. The phone rang a second time. Brandi picked it up and hit the reject button. After that the caller called two more times back to back. Finally, Brandi answered the phone.

"Hello!"

"Hi Brandi. How are ya?"

She couldn't believe her ears. It was Anthony. Why was he calling her when just two days previous she was almost blinded by the big ass rock he had given Jessica? "I'm fine Anthony. What's up?"

"Ya. Ya're wat's up? I wuz wonderin if I cud see ya."

"What about your girlfriend? Don't you think she would have a problem with that?" Brandi had to remind him that he had chosen another woman even though she desperately wanted to see him.

"Look Brandi, I can understan if ya say no but I really wanna see ya. Please."

"When and where Anthony. Only for a minute. I don't know what there is to say but I will see you and let you speak your peace."

"Lemme see. How bout 7:00 at my place? Can ya make it?" He asked.

"I'll be there." Brandi wondered what he wanted. He and Jessica couldn't have broken up. They were just together holding hands and smiling a couple of days ago. Maybe he just needed closure to move on. If that were the case, they both needed the same thing.

Brandi glimpsed at her watch. It was 5:20 already. That didn't leave her much time to get ready. She wondered where Jessica would be while she was at Anthony's house. After a quick shower, Brandi decided on a pair of jeans with a "V" neck top and heels. As she was leaving, Shemeka was coming in the door.

"Umph! Where are you headed?" Shemeka asked, looking her friend over from head to toe.

"Oh I just decided to ride out for a little while." She lied.

"I hope you are not going to the bar." Shemeka responded.

"No Meka. I am not going to the bar. Stop worrying so damn much. I'll be fine. Just catching some fresh air." She hugged her friend and left.

Once in the car, she thought while driving to Anthony's house. *I hated lying to Meka but I know she would have called me a damn fool if she knew I was going to meet Anthony. How in the hell can I explain to Meka why I am going when I don't even know myself? At least he is doing well and has a nice house and car. I should be the woman on his arms. Not Jessica.* She drove to Anthony's house thinking about how her life would be so different if she had stood by him. Instead she had turned him away for a gay ass doctor.

Brandi pulled in the driveway of the brick veneer, split-level house. She had driven by it plenty of nights wondering what Anthony was doing but not daring to stop. She stepped out of the car and walked up the sidewalk. The front door was open and Anthony stood in front of the full-length glass exterior door. He wore black sweats and no shirt. Brandi felt her heart skip a beat.

"Come on in. Wat wud ya like ta drink?" He asked Brandi as he stepped aside to allow her entrance.

"Gin and grapefruit juice will be fine." She answered. Brandi couldn't help but admire the well-kept house.

She observed the living room with its hard wood floor, the Persian rug, the beautiful paintings on the wall, and the home interior. The living room suit captivated her. White leather. It was many steps up from where Anthony had come from.

"Lemme git ya drink and I sho ya round."

"No! You don't have to. I'm only here because I thought you wanted to talk. So what's up?" She sat on the sofa and looked at Anthony. He'd been working out. He was so buff and he was more muscular than he had been when he was released.

Anthony sat on the couch beside Brandi and tried to put his arms around her but she pushed his arm away. "What's up Anthony?"

"Babe, I know things ain't go down right tween us. I hate dat shit. Ya pose ta be der fer a brotha. I mean like ya no Ima always feel ya Brandi."

"So what the hell is this Anthony? Is this an attempt to clear the air before you moved on with Jessica? We could have had this conversation on the telephone." She stood. "Go on with your fancy car and nice house and lil woman. You don't owe me an explanation. You don't owe me shit. In fact, I'm leaving." Brandi walked towards the door.

Anthony put his hand on Brandi's arm. "No Brandi. Wait a minna. I'm sorry. Don lev. I mean like seein ya da otha day just brung up des memories. I hafta keep Jessica round cuz she stood by me wen ya lef me. Ya know I'm feelin ya gurl."

Brandi looked at Anthony. She still loved him. She had never stopped. Knowing that she was vulnerable, Brandi began to feel uncomfortable. "I need to leave."

Anthony placed a hand on each of her shoulders before kissing her neck.

"No Anthony." She responded in a soft whisper. "Don't."

"I wan ya Brandi. It's been a long time." He took his right hand from her shoulder and lifted her chin. Anthony gently kissed her. Brandi closed her mouth at first; refusing his tongue but soon gave in to the passion and enjoyed the kiss.

"What do you want from me Anthony?" She questioned.

"I missed ya Brandi, and we wuz gud fore thins got crazy." He kissed her forehead.

"Anthony, it's not that I didn't want to stand by you. I hung in there with you for a long time. You kept getting in trouble and getting thrown in the hole. I was lonely. We couldn't have phone sex. I could only talk to you fifteen minutes a month. It was hard. I never stopped loving you. I always loved you. I never stopped." Tears rolled down her face.

Anthony wiped the tears before taking her hand in his. He led her to the bedroom. Brandi looked around the large bedroom with its hardwood floors. Black and white zebra design throw rugs matched the comforter that adorned the king size bed. The bed with its four high post had a white satin bench at the foot of it. Black and white sheer curtains allowed the sun to peep into the room.

Brandi allowed Anthony to lay her back on the bed and undress her. She remained quiet as he leaned over to suck her breast before undressing himself. He was rock hard and standing tall. He climbed into bed and instantly parted her legs. *Some things never change.* She thought. Anthony had never been a man who did a lot of foreplay. It had always bothered Brandi but she put up with it because she loved him and wanted to be with him.

"Is dis my pussy?" He asked as he stroked her. "Is it mine?"

"Yes Anthony. It has always been yours." Brandi answered.

Brandi enjoyed sex with Anthony. Her love for him is what made it special. Nothing so explosive that he was doing, but just being with him was enough to satisfy her. He pulled his dick out of her and stood.

"Suck it Brandi. I missed ya mouf on my dick."

She fell to her knees and took him in and out of her mouth while he moaned in pleasure.

"Ahh …daaay…am. Ya suckin my dick so gud. Yeah. Dat shit feel gud. Aww.. aww…yeah!" Before she knew it he had tightened his grip on her head and shoved his dick deeper down her throat as he exploded. She swallowed his juices before he collapsed on the bed.

Brandi was lost for words. She crawled into bed and lay in his arms. Suddenly she wondered about Jessica. *Where the hell is Jessica? Is he going to break up with Jessica and get back with me where he belongs? What in the world will Rhonda and Meka say? They never cared for Anthony in the first place.*

Anthony broke the silence. "Dat wuz gud Brandi. Dat's sum gud pussy ya walkin round wit tween ya legs but dem dam lips is hell. Next time Ima hafta hook ya up rite."

"So what now?" She questioned.

"Well now…" He sat up in bed. "I gotta get cleaned up so I can get outta here. I gotta take a load out tonite. Wanna join me in da shower?"

"Nah! You go ahead. I will just take a quick wash up and get on back to the house." Brandi felt like a fourteen-karat fool.

"Okay." Anthony agreed. "Ya can use the bathroom down da hall."

Brandi went to the hall bathroom. She took a washcloth from the laundry room and filled the sink with water. *How do you wash away stupid? He didn't mention us being together. He didn't mention Jessica. I don't know whom in the hell he thinks I am. I will not be his damn backdoor whore. Fuck that shit!*

After Brandi cleaned up, she put her washcloth in the dirty clothes hamper and walked back to the bedroom. She stuck her head in the bathroom where Anthony was singing off key in the shower. "All right Anthony. I'm outta here."

"Ok." He stopped singing. "Thanks.

Brandi walked out of the house locking and closing the door behind her. *Thanks?? That's all I get is a damn thanks? I feel used like hell. The girls can never know about this shit. What in the hell possessed me to give that bastard the time of day? He's moved on. I need to do the same. I can't put my life on hold waiting on him to decide how he is going to fit me in and I most definitely can't be his whore. He treated me like a piece of poor white trash. Fuck him!*

Chapter 9

Rhonda sat in the family room with her feet resting on the ottoman. *That damn Victor Newman is hell!* She thought to herself while she enjoyed watching her favorite soap opera. She had been a fan of 'The Young and the Restless' every since she could remember.

Bernard was at work; Dean at school and it was Nard's second day at daycare. It hadn't been easy to let go of Nard. He was such a sweet toddler. He hadn't started talking yet and kept mostly to himself. He didn't seem to mind when Dean was being the pestering sister, but Bernard felt that he needed to be in daycare to help him with social skills.

Oh shit! Jack Abbott should know by now who he is messing with, she thought. *Victor doesn't play.* When she leaned forward to witness the confrontation between her favorite rivals, the intercom rang. *Damn!* She said aloud while getting up. She pushed the button on the wall to her right.

"Yes?"

"UPS with a delivery for Mrs. Rhonda Simpson." The man answered.

"One minute please." Rhonda responded.

Rhonda went to the door and signed for the package. The man handed her a medium sized package wrapped in bright red paper with red and white ribbon. She gave the man a tip and walked back to the family room wondering who could have possibly sent her a gift. *Oh!* She thought. *Bernard is trying to make up for falling asleep on me last night.*

When she opened the box, there was a pair of red crotchless panties trimmed in black lace on top of tissue paper. *Wow!* She opened the tissue paper to see what else was in the box. There was a beautiful red negligee to match the panties, a red and black lace choker, lace gloves and a small stick with a feather on the tip. Rhonda smiled as she picked up the note in the bottom of the box. She unfolded the note.

"Oh my God!" She mumbled. "Nikki!" Rhonda stumbled backwards and sat on the chair to read the note.

Baby,

Mama is getting anxious. I can close my eyes right now and see you in this sexy red gown. Red is your color. You do know that don't you? I want you to wear it when I get home. It won't be long and we will be seeing each other. I don't mean for you to wear this for your lame ass husband. I will know if you do. And I will know if he puts his mouth on my damn cookie. If you know what's good for you then you will keep my fuckin cookie fresh for me. Mmm...mmm...mmm...mmm...Wah! Mama just doesn't want to have to fuck you up. Please! Please! Please! Baby please don't ever stop loving me. We are for life. I love you forever and always. You are mine and I am yours.

Nikki Boo.

Rhonda tore the letter into small pieces before tearing up the box and the pretty paper that was in it. She went to the trash can and moved some things around so the letter and packaging would be at the bottom of the trash can. Afterwards she took the negligee and panties to her room and placed them in the bottom of one of her drawers.

That bitch has to have connections in Brooksville. She has to. How the fuck did she get her hands on this shit? Why the hell does she keep eluding to the fact that she may be getting out soon? She's probably just trying to intimidate me. Fuck her. That bitch is not getting out of there any time soon.

'The Young and The Restless' was still on but Rhonda was no longer interested in watching her favorite soap opera. She was too deep in thought. *How was Nikki able to get a package to me? Who in the hell has she conned? Can she talk them into coming here? What does she want? This has to stop and I mean now. I haven't seen that lunatic in years but I am going to have to go to Brooksville.*

Rhonda was beside herself, not understanding what Nikki's motive was. Did she suddenly want to cause trouble or what? Dean's bus wouldn't come for three and a half hours so she had time. Nard wouldn't be home until later. His dad always picked him up from daycare after he got off work. She ruffled through her closet and found something suitable to wear to the institution.

The closer she got to Brooksville, the more nervous Rhonda got. The trip across town was only twenty minutes from her house but it seemed as if she had driven for hours. She knew better than to confront Nikki. Instead, she would plead with the lunatic to leave her alone and stop sending unwanted gifts to her house.

A plump white lady with gray hair and eyeglasses hanging down on her nose sat behind a glass petition. "May I help you?"

"Yes you may. I am here to visit Nicole Harris."

She handed Rhonda a clipboard. "You'll need to sign in."

Rhonda took the visitors log. She hesitated about signing in. She didn't want to put her name on the log but she didn't see where she had much choice. What if she put a false name and then they asked for ID? She couldn't take a chance on that, especially since there was a security guard standing in the corner watching her. After signing her name, she gave the clipboard back to the receptionist.

"Let's see…lunch is over. Nicole is probably in the dayroom. Make a left here and go down the hall until you come to green tile. Hang a right there and the dayroom will be two doors down on the right."

"Thank you!" Rhonda answered. She walked to the dayroom feeling like she was walking through the gates of hell. When she walked into the dayroom the patients were engaged. Some sat at a table playing cards, some stood in various parts of the room talking to themselves, and some doodled with crayons and paper. One woman used her finger to make circular motions on the wall. Nikki sat in a chair looking at a magazine.

When she looked up and saw Rhonda walking towards her, she smiled and stood. The two embraced. Nikki whispered in Rhonda's ear. "I knew you would come to Mama."

Rhonda pulled back from her. "We need to talk Nikki. Is there somewhere we can go? Is there a patio or something?"

"We can go to my room. I just have to let them know where I will be. They only lock us in our room at night." The two women walked over to Lance who was standing near the door as if he were a guard on post. He had been forced to work a double since the nurse who was scheduled to work had a sick child.

"Sir." Nikki always spoke to Lance in a way that no one would ever suspect the two were having sex on a regular basis. "I'll be in my room. My guest and I have to discuss some legalities concerning my children." It was the first time Lance had heard Nikki mention the children.

"That will be fine." He answered.

"Gee! Thanks Sir." She turned to Rhonda. "Follow me."

The two walked down the hall to Nikki's room. Rhonda began to relax after seeing how calm Nikki was. Once they were in the room,

Nikki sat on the bed. She patted the spot beside her with her left hand. "Have a seat Rhonda. What's on your mind? I'm glad you came to see me."

"No! I'll stand. This shouldn't take long." Rhonda remarked.

Nikki smiled. "Did you get your gift from Mama?"

"Yes, Nikki. I did get it. That's why I am here." Rhonda decided to have a seat on the bed. Nikki was being calm and she didn't want to rock the boat. "Nikki you have to stop. I'm serious. Bernard could have been home and signed for that package. Then what? How would I have explained it?"

"It was just a gift. I saw it in a magazine and wanted you to have it. Don't you remember how I love seeing you in red?" Nikki placed her left hand on Rhonda's thigh and even though she wanted to remove it, she dared not.

"Thank you. I appreciate it. I just don't want any problems."

Rhonda could feel as Nikki dug her fingernails deeper and deeper into her skin. "There won't be any motherfuckin problems as long as you don't spoil things Bitch! I don't give a damn about your limp dick husband." She removed her hand from Rhonda's thigh.

Rhonda glanced at her thigh and saw that the skin was broken. She rubbed her thigh and stood. Nikki stood in front of her and raised Rhonda's dress in an attempt to put her hands in Rhonda's panties.

"Stop!" Rhonda told her. "Don't do that shit!" She put her hand on top of Nikki's hand to stop her. "Please Nikki. Don't do this!"

Nikki used the heel of her foot to try to close the door. The door was stopped by Lance who had just walked up. Rhonda felt a sense of relief until she realized that Nikki wasn't fazed by his presence.

"Is everything okay Ladies?" He questioned.

"She was about to leave. Stand there at the door for a minute." Nikki answered without removing her hand. She shoved her middle finger hard into Rhonda. "Who does this fuckin cookie belong to?" Nikki was forceful and hurting Rhonda.

"Stop Nikki. You're hurting me." Rhonda pleaded. She glanced towards the door and noticed Lance gazing at them. *Damn! What the hell is his problem? Why isn't he taking control of this situation? The bitch is not even trying to stop her.*

Nikki took her hand out of Rhonda's panties and pushed her back until she was on the bed. Rhonda looked pleadingly at Lance. *Surely he will intervene now.*

"Nikki I have to go. No one is home to let the kids in."

Lance never moved. *What's his fuckin problem?* Rhonda thought. *He acts more like a damn patient than an employee.*

Nikki tried to kiss Rhonda. When she resisted, Nikki spoke to her in a deep voice. "Don't fuckin make Mama mad. Do you understand?" She grabbed Rhonda's chin and tried again. Rhonda returned the kiss in hopes that Nikki would let her leave. Once the kiss was over she tried to leave. Nikki grabbed her and pulled her into a strong embrace. "I won't let you spoil it." She held her tighter. "I hope you understand. This is my damn cookie. All mine and no one else can have any. Keep that cookie fresh for Mama."

Rhonda shook herself free and ran past Lance. She ran past the receptionist desk without signing out. Once she was safely in her car, she began to cry. *She's crazy. That bitch is crazy as hell. What in the hell made me think I could reason with that fool?* She cranked her car up. *Who the hell was that son-of-a-bitch watching us like that? He's probably her damn connection to the outside world with his dumb ass. I bet that's how she is able to send shit to me but he better not let me find out or I will have his ass fired.*

Chapter 10

Lance didn't know what to think except that Nikki was crazy out of her head and exactly where she belonged. He felt sorry for her visitor. *Who was that woman?* He asked himself. *I wonder what Nikki has on her. She looked scared as hell but there was nothing I could do for her.* He felt bad but there was no way in hell that he would get into the middle of anything Nikki had going on. He walked back to the day room. Nikki had returned to her previous spot.

"Excuse me Sir. May I see you for a minute?" She waved her arm in the air and motioned for Lance to come her way.

"Yes Ma'am. What can I do for you?" He asked Nikki.

"Meet me in my room in ten minutes." She whispered in a soft voice.

"I don't think that's a good idea. Someone may notice." He whispered back.

"I didn't ask you if it was a good idea Motherfucka. Just do it." This time her voice was raised above a whisper. "Don't fuckin play with me. What the hell is wrong with you?"

"I'll be there." Lance agreed. Nikki wasn't giving him much choice. He didn't know what she was capable of. He didn't want to upset her because she had proven she was nothing to play with. He gave her time to get to her room before telling the receptionist he was taking his break. After making sure no one was looking, he slipped into Nikki's room.

Upon entering her room, he found Nikki on her bed in a fetal position rocking back and forth. He was a little nervous. It was clear to him that this woman he had fallen in love with was dealing with some issues. He wondered if she was still taking her medicine or if she had somehow been able to dispose of it. "Nikki, I'm here. What's so urgent? I can't stay too long. I am on break."

Nikki uncurled her body and stood. "Motherfucka, did I ask you how long you had? DID I? NO I DIDN'T, BECAUSE I DON'T GIVE A FUCK. I'm telling you man. If you don't get me out of here soon something bad is going to happen. You are not going to like the way it goes down. Trust me Lance." She pointed her finger in his face. "It won't be pretty."

"Baby I've been working on this plan and I am about to have it perfect. Give me just a little more time. It's going to happen. I know I been asking you to be patient, but bare with me just a little bit longer."

"I'm sorry Lance. I don't mean to be ugly. It's just that you don't understand. I am about to go crazy up in this bitch. I know you will get me out of here soon. I would give you a hug but I don't want to take a chance on anybody walking by here and seeing us."

"I know. You have always been discreet and I appreciate that. I'm going to look out for you Nikki. I really care for you." Lance wasn't lying. He had developed feelings for Nikki. She was a great sex partner and when she was on her medication she had great conversation. He knew it was wrong with him being a married man but he had never had a woman as freaky as Nikki. She wasn't gay because she did such a splendid job of taking care of him and his needs. However, some of the things he had witnessed caused him to wonder if she was bi-sexual.

"Lance, that was my friend Rhonda who visited with me earlier. She used to belong to me before I came into this place. Her cookie is one of the sweetest I've ever eaten. It tastes like pure sugar. She acts like she has forgotten about me since I have been in here. I need to get out of here so I can remind her of the fact that no one can take care of her like Mama can. I don't think she remembers."

Lance didn't know how to respond to that. He was speechless.

"I'm glad you didn't try to come between us Lance." She continued. "My baby is very special to me. And that cookie has my name on it. But you know that you are also mine don't you? That dick belongs to me and if you ever give it away I don't know what I'd do. I've grown to care about you. Thanks for all you have done for me. I appreciate you. Now get out of here before somebody starts looking for you." She kissed Lance on the forehead and he left.

****

Rhonda arrived home thirty minutes before Dean's bus was scheduled to arrive. She kicked her shoes off and stretched out in the recliner. *What the hell is Nikki up to?* She asked herself. *I know that damn man is the one who helped her get mail out to me with his flicked ass. He should be a damn patient.*

Just as she had gotten comfortable Bernard walked in with Nard. The child walked past Rhonda and took four of Dean's pencils off the table. Bernard watched as his son sat on the floor and lined the pencils.

"What's up?" Rhonda asked him. "You're early. Was Nard not feeling well or something?"

"No! That's not it. Where have you been? The daycare tried to call you but they were unable to reach you. They said they needed to talk to a parent. Since it was the end of the day anyway, I asked my assistant to watch the class."

"I was tired of hanging around the house." She lied. "So I jumped in the car and took a little stroll. I thought I'd get some fresh air." She walked to where Nard was playing with the pencils.

"Come here fella. What seems to be the problem?"

The child continued to play with the pencils as if Rhonda hadn't spoken.

"Nard! Nard!" She called a couple of times but he was fixated on the pencils. "Okay." Rhonda gave up. "You never pay me any attention anyway." She turned to her husband. "So what's up? Why did they need to talk to a parent?"

They are concerned about Nard. He doesn't play or socialize with the other children. He doesn't talk and he won't respond when they call his name. You see how he was just a minute ago when you called out to him. The daycare feels like we should have him tested."

"Tested for what? The child doesn't want to be bothered. I am the same way at times so I can relate.

"I don't know Baby." Bernard sat on the chair. "Maybe we should have him checked out. It wouldn't hurt anything. That way we will know for certain if anything is wrong."

Rhonda didn't protest. "Alright. We'll have him tested. I will make an appointment for him. I know it is a waste of time but if it will ease your mind lets do it. The child is just lazy. When he has something to say, he will say it.

"Thanks Babe."

Rhonda's cell phone rang. She looked at it but didn't recognize the number of the caller. "Hello." There was definitely no mistaking who the caller was.

She held the cell phone in her hand while she listened. "Hi Sexy. Did you enjoy that tongue action today? Next time you come, I am going to stick my finger in your cookie. Would you like that?"

Bernard had gotten up and was standing near Rhonda. She couldn't freely talk and definitely didn't want him to know she had visited Nikki at Brooksville. "No. I wouldn't care for any today. Thanks for calling." She answered.

"Bitch you better not hang up this damn phone." Nikki's voice blared through the phone. "I'm not finish talking to your ass. Are you going to let me eat my cookie or what?"

Rhonda knew that if she hung up the phone it would send Nikki spiraling into a rage. "Well actually I already have plenty at this time. Maybe some other time."

"Your limp dick husband better not be fuckin with my cookie. I tell you that. When are you coming to see Mama again?" Nikki questioned.

Never! She wanted to scream but she knew better. "I appreciate it. Have a good day." Rhonda ended the call. She pushed the talk button on her cell phone to pull up her list of recent calls. She clicked on the telephone number Nikki had just called from and pressed options. Scrolling down the list of options, she stopped at the one that read *add to reject list.* She pressed the button. When prompted, *Are you sure you want to add this number?* She pressed *yes.* Silently she spoke to herself. *HELL YES!!!*

Chapter 11

Karen dreaded going into Brooksville. It was her day off and she had not had two days off in a row for quite some time. She wanted to go visit her sister and spend time with her two nieces. Karen knew she didn't have a choice now as to how to spend the time. It would have been better if she hadn't even answered the telephone when Lance called. He sounded so serious. *Karen, this is Lance. You need to meet me in Nikki's room shortly after midnight. It's imperative that we both be there. Don't ask what's going on. You will see when you get there. I can't explain right now. Just make sure you are there on time. You know that Nikki doesn't have patience. Please! If you don't come, I don't know what she might do but I know there will be hell to pay.*

"I'll be there!" She had told him. Now she was rethinking that decision. *What the hell have those two cooked up now? I'm not in for that threesome shit. I don't even like Lance with his arrogant ass. Getting involved with Nikki was the biggest mistake of my life. Damn Erik! I hate his gay ass. He's the reason all of this bullshit happened.*

Karen walked in and was greeted by Ms. Covington. "Hey there Missy. Thought you were off tonight. What are you doing here?"

I'm going out of town in the morning and need something I had loaned to Lance."

"What did you loan him Honey? Some money?"

Ms. Covington had always been a nosey woman but she didn't mean any harm. Everybody figured she needed somebody's business to meddle in as a distraction to take her mind off her daughter.

"I loaned him my GPS. I can't very well leave town without my GPS. Especially since I don't know where I am going." Karen answered.

"Yep. You are going to need that. I would hate for you to be lost out there Honey. People are so bad these days. It's better to be safe than to be sorry." Ms. Covington picked up a clipboard and flipped through some charts.

Karen used the opportunity to slip away and meet Lance in Nikki's room. She stood outside room #341 so nervous she thought her heart would jump out of her chest. She tapped lightly on the door and Lance opened it to let her in.

"Come on in Baby." Nikki said. "Did Lance tell you why Mama needs you?"

"No." She answered. "He just said to be here. So what's going on? I had made plans to go out of town. What is so urgent that I had to cancel my plans and be here?"

Nikki slid over and made room for Karen to sat on the bed beside her. Karen sat reluctantly.

"Baby, it's time for Mama to get out of here. I've been in here too long and I can't do it any longer. I'm leaving Thursday."

Karen sighed a breath of relief. Finally, Nikki was getting out of her hair. Out of her hair and out of her life. She could come to work without Nikki making demands on her. She felt like shouting. She was so excited she could hardly contain herself but she had to. She knew that Nikki wasn't gone yet so she had to play the role.

"I'm sorry Nikki. I know this will be a good thing for you but I am truly going to miss you. I really have enjoyed you."

"No fool! They are not letting me out. Lance is helping me to escape."

"What?" Karen looked at Lance who was standing quietly in the corner. "How is he going to do that? If anybody catches yall they will…"

"Shhh! Quiet!" Nikki interrupted her. "It's not y'all. It's us. And who is going to catch us. With the three of us working together we can make sure things go off without a hitch."

"What are you talking about, the three of us?" Karen protested. "I'm not having anything to do with this. I won't tell anybody about it but I'm not going to have a part of it."

Nikki threw her head back and laughed a wicked laugh. "Now sweetness you don't even know what Mama needs for you to do. I love you and I know that you aren't going to disappoint me. You wouldn't do Mama like that would you?" Nikki continued to laugh.

Karen didn't know whether Nikki was up to something or if she had lost the rest of whatever was left of her brain. "Nikki, I can't be involved in this mess. I need my job. Who is going to pay my bills? I can't take any chances. I'm sorry."

Before Karen could stand up, Nikki leaned across the bed and pushed her on her back. She rolled over on top of Karen and put both hands around her neck while Lance watched quietly. Karen gasped as Nikki applied pressure. Her head bobbed back and forth on the bed while Nikki applied more pressure. She attempted to remove Nikki's hand from her throat.

"I will kill you Bitch! I have been good to you. I will kill your fuckin Latino ass and step right over your dead body to get out of this motherfucker. Do you understand me?"

Karen tried to nod her head in agreement. When Nikki let go of her she stood and tried to clear her throat as she rubbed her neck. "What do you want me to do? Why are you dragging me into this?" Karen questioned.

In a flash and without warning, Nikki backhanded her across the face. "What I tell you about that? You don't question me. Who in the hell do you think you are? Stand your ass there and listen."

Karen stood there silently thanking God that she had tomorrow off. Nikki had hit her pretty hard and she felt for sure that she would be bruised by morning.

"Oh my goodness. Why in the hell did you make me do that? Come here Boo. You know Mama loves you. I wish you wouldn't upset Mama like that. Come on. Come on over here to Mama."

Karen slowly walked to Nikki. *I'll be so damn glad to see this bitch gone that I don't know what to do. Putting her damn hands in my face. I hate her!*

She kissed Karen on the forehead. "I'm so sorry Baby but you are going to have to learn how to be good. You just have to. Mama hurt her hand trying to chastise you. I don't like to do that. You keep upsetting Mama. Don't do that. I might accidentally hurt you one day." She licked the side of Karen's face. "Now let me tell you how things are going to go down. Your job is not going to be in jeopardy. Mama loves you too much to do that to you."

Thank goodness. At least the fool is talking with a little bit of sense now.

Lance is getting me out of here." Nikki continued. "Everything is almost set. He just doesn't have a place for me to go when I get out. That's where you come in. I'm going to have to hang out with you at your place for a little while until we can make other arrangements. Mama really needs your help on this one."

Karen felt sick to her stomach. She didn't want Nikki in her home. *Why in the hell can't Lance find her a place with his simple punk ass?* "I don't know Nikki. People are in and out of my house all the time. And you know they will have your face plastered all over the news. You'll get caught and how will I be able to explain that?" She glanced over towards Lance whom had not opened his mouth. Although he was scared of Nikki, didn't the mere fact that he was a man require him to have some balls?

"Don't worry about that Baby. It will be ok. I love you and I can't wait to eat my juicy fruit on the regular."

Karen was speechless. *Oh my goodness. There has to be a way to get out of this. Nikki is crazy as hell. How can I have that lunatic hiding out at my house? There has to be another alternative.* She walked over to where Lance was standing. "Don't you think it would be better if we tried to find her a lil house outside of the city limits? I just think it is too risky to have her here in town. I don't want her to get out, only to get caught again. It doesn't seem like you have thought this thing out clearly." Her eyes pleaded for his agreement.

"No! Your place is goanna be perfect. It was not my idea. It was Nikki's. She knows what she is doing." Lance moved to where Nikki was standing and put his arms around her. "As far as I am concerned, it's settled. Nikki will stay at your house until we can find more permanent placement."

Damn! I'm sick as hell. It is useless to protest. They both have their minds made up. I feel sick to my damn stomach.

"Tomorrow night." Lance told her. "It's going down tomorrow night. I will get in touch with you to go over the details. Right now I have to move about the halls. You know how Miss. Covington is with her nosey ass."

"Yeah I know. I have to leave too." Karen said. "Make sure the coast is clear for me." Karen needed to get out of there before she broke down.

"I know you aren't leaving without giving me that tongue are you?" Nikki asked.

Lance wasn't sure if the question was directed to him or Karen but he gave Nikki a wet tongue kiss while Karen watched.

"Now come get yours." Nikki licked her lips and motioned for Karen to come forward. She cuffed Karen's breast before kissing her. When Karen walked towards the door, Nikki grabbed her arm. "Keep that fruit juicy. Mama can't wait to bite into it tomorrow night."

When Karen got to her car she was so nervous that she couldn't steady her hands enough to unlock the car door. She knelt beside her car and cried into her hands. *What am I going to do? I can't take this shit. And if I can't take it now, how in the hell am I going to take it when she moves in. Lord please don't let her be with me long.*

Karen felt a hand on her shoulder. She looked up to see Lance standing over her. "I looked out and saw your car in the parking lot. Are you okay Karen? I'm sorry about the way everything unfolded in there but I can't cross Nikki. I love her." He took Karen's hand to help her up.

"What? Love her? You can't be that big of a fool. Nikki is crazy. She doesn't give a damn about you. You are just a means to an end. I thought you had more sense than that. You should be locked up right along with her if you are stupid enough to think she can ever love you."

"Go home Karen. I just came out to check on you. Nikki will be at your place tomorrow night. I will need for you to leave your car unlocked with the keys under the mat. Also leave your address under the mat."

"What the hell do you need my keys for?" Karen questioned.

"Just do as you are told woman! Remember that Nikki could cause you to have to go to the unemployment line. After you leave the keys in the car, walk to Denny's. They stay open 24 hours. Make sure to talk to the waitress or do something to make sure she remembers you were there. That within itself will clear you because you will have an alibi for when Nikki escapes. "Oh yeah! Make sure to leave your back door unlocked. Nikki should be there by 1:15 a.m. Any questions?"

"No Lance. No questions." Karen unlocked the door and got in her car. She rolled the window down. "You are one more spineless ass man. Good bye." She sped away.

Chapter 12

Brandi felt like she must be losing it. Why else would she find herself back in front of Anthony's house? Was he seriously drawing her like a magnet or was it Shemeka's fault?

When Meka asked the girls to join her for drinks last night, neither was prepared for the conversation.

"Y'all my gals and I love ya." She had told them. "So y'all need to know that I have finally found me a house that I am going to buy."

Brandi was saddened to hear the news. She was happy for Meka but she and Meka had been each other's rock. They had helped each other to hold it together. What would she do without her rock?

Rhonda was excited to hear the news. "We'll have to do a house warming for you. That's great news. Tell us about the house you've found. How big is it?"

"Not too big. It has three bedrooms, kitchen, den, living room, and one and a half baths." Meka answered.

"That's what's up!" Rhonda responded. "When can we see it?"

"If you had your laptop with you, you could go online and see it now." She answered.

"Online? I don't want to see it online. I want to step my foot in the door."

Brandi sat silently. She wasn't ready for Meka to leave her. She at least needed time for the idea to sink in.

"Oh! Okay." Meka told her. "You can step your foot inside. When do you want to come to Florida?"

"Florida?" Rhonda and Brandi exclaimed in unison.

"Stop playing Meka." Brandi told her. "You know damn well you are not moving your ass to Florida."

"Yes I am. It'll be good. I need a change. Yall are my gals and I would never do this if I didn't think it was a good move. This is something I have to do for me. I hope you understand."

"I'm not going to say I understand. I know you have dealt with a lot. Things that would probably still have me totally freaked out." Rhonda answered. "So even though I don't understand, I will support you in your decision."

Brandi ordered another Bahama Mama. "I'll have to think about it." She poked her lip out as if she was pouting. There was really nothing to think about. Shemeka was moving out of town and things were about to change. With her world becoming smaller, she didn't have much choice but to agree to meet with Anthony when he called.

Anthony still loves me. She rationalized to keep from feeling stupid. *Otherwise he wouldn't keep calling me. I wonder why Jessica is never around. I thought they were so happily engaged. They can't be all that. Something must have happened. Well he is supposed to be mine anyway.*

Brandi stepped out of her Camry and walked to the door. Anthony came to the door in a pair of sweatpants and no shirt. "Come on in Brandi, I missed ya." He kissed her on the cheek. "I really have been missin ya gurl."

She walked over to the chaise lounger and sat down. "What about Jessica, Ant? What's up with that?"

Anthony walked over to Brandi and stood in front of her. "Ba, she ain't no problum. I hafta be nice to hur cuz she waz der fer me wen ya kicked a brotha to da curb. Wat ya speck fer me ta do? I'm always gon be feelin ya. I told ya dat da las time ya wuz here."

Brandi was vulnerable to Anthony. She never stopped loving him. Although he was a straight up street dude, there were moments when he made her feel like the most special and loved woman in the world.

"Wat ya like ta drink?" Anthony asked her as he walked to the wrap around bar.

"Let me try gin and juice today." Brandi kicked off her shoes while she surveyed the room. Anthony had done very well with truck driving. He was a prime example that there is life after prison. Anthony handed Brandi the drink before kissing her and taking a seat.

"Gurl, wat ya wearin unda dat dress?"

"What do you think I'm wearing? You know what I wear. I have on thongs."

"I no but I just wanna see. Kick dose thins off and lay back an open dem legs for daddy. Spread em wide and close ya eyes."

Brandi did as Anthony asked her. She slid out of her black lace thongs and relaxed on the chaise lounge chair with knees bent. She spread her legs and closed her eyes. Brandi could feel herself getting moist as she waited to feel his mouth on her. Instead, he kissed her inner thighs. She loved that he was teasing her, making her wait for the pleasure. Suddenly she felt him put something between her legs and push her legs closed.

What the hell? Did he write me a note or something? He's tripping.

"You can open your eyes now." Anthony sat on the side of the bed.

Brandi opened her eyes and removed the paper from between her legs. She could recognize that it was a check. She unfolded the check and gasped. The check from Logan Transit was made payable to Anthony

Woodruff. "What are you doing Anthony? Why did you give me this check?"

"I see dat ya happy wit da check. It's yours. Go shoppin. Buy anythin ya want. Git some jeans fer dat phatt ass. I already signed it. Dis is yo day."

Brandi couldn't believe it. Anthony must be doing even better than she thought. How else could he afford to sign over a whole paycheck to her? "Are you sure? Do you really mean this whole check is mine to spend any way I want? What's up with that? What's the catch?"

"Nunthin up wit dat. I wanna make ya happy and I wan ya ta look good. Is anythin wrong with dat? I neva stop carin bout ya." He kissed Brandi.

"I love you Anthony." She leaned down to pick up her thongs off the floor before taking his hand and standing. "Let's finish this discussion in the bedroom."

Anthony let her lead him down the corridor. Before they reached the master bedroom, the doorbell rang.

"DAMN!" Anthony exclaimed. "Go head and git it ready fer me. I will get rid of whoeva at da door.

Brandi scurried on to the bedroom while Anthony answered the door. "Who is it?' He asked.

"Redd!"

Anthony quickly opened the door. What da fuck ya doin here man? Don ya see dat I got company? Ya know I don roll like dat."

"I'm sorry Dawg, but I been hearing some shit on the streets that I think you should know about. You know that I never would have stopped with Brandi's car out there. This is some deep shit man. We gotta talk."

"Anthony." Brandi called out from the bedroom. "Did you forget about me?"

"Fix ya a drink man and leme take care of dis. It won take but a minute." He walked down the corridor and into the bedroom.

Brandi had herself positioned at the foot of the bed on her hands and knees with her ass turned up in the air. Immediately he grabbed his crotch and walked over to her. He gently tapped her ass with his hand. "Babe, I'm sorry. Sumthin has come up dat I need ta take care of. I'll make it up ta ya. I'm sorry."

"Something more important than me? Brandi turned over and sat on the bed as if she were pouting. She folded her arms and pushed her bottom lip out before slowly getting back into her clothes. "Well I guess I can use this time to get that shopping done. Go on and take care of your business."

After she was dressed, Anthony walked her to the door. Redd was seated at the bar. "What's up Brandi?" He nodded his head at her.

"Hey Redd." She responded as she strolled on towards the door. "Anthony!" She whispered. "What the hell is Redd doing here? You know that he's nothing but a piece of shit."

"Nah Boo. It's not like dat. Redd's cool, He looked out fer a brotha wen I was down. You know how da shit goes. Outta sight outta mind. I did a lot fer des motherfuckas round here but when a brotha hit the joint, people ferget. Not Redd. He put a few dollars on my books from time ta time and he came ta visit a brotha eva now and den. He's cool."

Brandi opened the door. "Ok. If you say so. Watch your back though because I don't trust him." Anthony kissed her before she got in her car and drove away,

Chapter 13

It was five minutes past midnight and Karen felt like her nerves were all over the place. She parked her car at Brooksville and checked out her surroundings. Once she decided everything was clear, she placed her keys under the mat and headed to Denny's. She wished she didn't have to be a part of this escape thing. If only she had not given in to Nikki that night. It was all Erik's fault. Gay ass bitch. Why the hell did he even allow her to fall in love with him, knowing he was on the down low? He could have kept his shit in the closet and stayed the hell out of her life.

"Dining alone?" The hostess asked Karen.

"Yeah. I couldn't sleep. Man problems. Thought I'd have a bite to eat. Feed my troubles."

"Right this way. Follow me."

The restaurant was not too crowded. *Great! The less people here the better chance of my being noticed.*

"How's this?" The hostess asked after taking Karen to a small table in the corner.

"This is fine. Thank you."

"Your waitress will be right with you. Enjoy your meal."

When the hostess walked away Karen looked at the menu. She knew she had to order something but how in the hell could she hold anything on her stomach knowing she would be going home to Nikki. She looked at her watch. *Damn! Wonder if it's going down right now? Lance is going to have to do some major manipulations in order to pull this shit off. Why the hell is that fool jeopardizing his job for Nikki? He can't love her that much. Not the way she transforms his punk ass into her lil puppet on a string.* The waitress interrupted her thoughts.

"Hi. I'm Jana. I'll be your waitress. What can I get you to drink?"

"Coffee please. Decaf."

"Decaf coming right up. Have you decided what you'd like to eat or do you need a little more time to look over the menu?" The waitress was a short, stubby white woman with red hair.

"I'm ready to order. I'll have a BLT on toast with a side of hash browns." Karen was sure the waitress could hear her heart pounding. She was nervous. What if something went wrong? What if they got caught?

The waitress wrote on her tablet. "I'll be right back. I'm going to start a fresh pot of decaf. It won't take long.

"Thanks." Karen responded. *What about my damn car? If Lance gets caught sneaking Nikki out of there and they see my car, then I am toast. They know I am not working. How the hell can I explain this shit I let myself get caught up in? What if they figure out that I am in on the escape? If Lance gets caught I know that his stupid ass will talk. I never should have gone along with this. What was I thinking? Right. I wasn't thinking. As soon as I get my food, I'm out of here.*

Karen had all kinds of thoughts dancing around in her head when the waitress returned with her a cup of coffee. "Your food should be just about ready. I'll check on it."

She put cream and sugar in her coffee. She had only taken a few sips of her coffee when the waitress came back with her food. She sat the plate on the table. "Here you go. Can I get anything else for you?"

"No." Karen answered. "I'm fine, Thanks." *I need to hurry up and get the hell out of here so I can find out what is going on.* Karen quickly gulped her sandwich down. After leaving a tip on the table she paid for her meal. She used a credit card as further proof that she was at Denny's during the time of Nikki's attempted escape.

Karen exited the restaurant and crossed the street. A car approached her with its high beam headlights on. She recognized Lance as the driver. He pulled up beside her. "Get in!"

Karen opened the passenger door and climbed in the car. "What happened? Where's Nikki? Did you do it? Did you get her out of there? She was nervous and asking one question after another.

"Whoa! Slow your ass down." Lance told her.

"Everything is fine. Nosey ass Ms. Covington almost got in the way but she got a call that her daughter was in the hospital. Somebody beat her up I think. Nikki is at your house waiting for us. Nobody knows that she is gone yet. I am going to drop you off at home and then I need to get back to work."

"Oh my goodness Lance." She looked at him sitting behind the wheel so nonchalant like he hadn't just committed a damn crime. Acting like it was all in a days' work. Hell! His stupid ass needed a bed next to Nikki. "You just don't understand what kind of a position you have put me in. I don't know if I can pull this off or not. I'm afraid that if anybody asks me anything I will crack. No lie. I'm nervous as hell."

Lance slowed the car down and pulled to the side of the road. "Listen Karen. Get your damn self together. Why would anybody ask you anything? You didn't even work tonight. You are off the hook unless you blow it for yourself and in that case it's on you."

He pulled the car back onto the road. "Once you are home, have a drink and relax. Nikki is waiting for you. I won't be over for a few days but I'll be in touch through the pre-paid phone I gave Nikki. If you have any kind of emergency, call me from that phone only. Understand?"

"Yes Lance. I understand. It's you who don't understand."

Lance pulled into Karen's driveway. She sat quietly. "Ok." He told her. "This is your house. What are you waiting on? Get out! Damn! I got to get back to work. Why are you not moving?" He got out of his car and walked to the passenger side. As soon as he placed his hand on the door, he felt another hand on top of his. He grabbed his chest. "SHIT! You scared the hell out of me Nikki. I didn't see you. Where did you come from?"

"I'm sorry. I was waiting behind that tree. Is everything ok?" She inquired.

"Yes! Everything is fine. I was just helping Karen out of the car." He answered.

"Thanks, but I'll get her." Nikki opened the door. Karen's heart was racing. "Welcome Baby. I've been waiting for my fruit." Nikki leaned into the car and kissed Karen on the lips before taking her by the hand. "Come on. I'm so ready for you." Karen slowly removed herself from the car.

"I need to go." Lance said as he got back into the car. "I'll be in touch later."

"Bye Sexy.' Nikki answered. "Thanks for everything. I knew you wouldn't spoil it." He drove away with the two women standing in the driveway.

"You can go in Nikki. I will be in shortly. I need a minute to get myself together." She was not ready to accept that she was stuck with Nikki for a while.

"What the hell did you say? You need a minute to get yourself together? For what? Are you not fuckin glad to see Mama? Is there a damn problem?" Nikki asked angrily.

"No Mama. I'm glad to see you. Let's go in."

Nikki smiled. "Ok because I'm hungry and I want my fruit." She tried to put her hands in Karen's pants while they walked into the house. Karen stopped her.

"Wait. Not tonight. I'm really tired."

"Not tonight huh?" Nikki chuckled. "Your motherfuckin ass is too tired. Right?"

"Yes Mama. I'm tired." Karen answered with hesitation.

At that moment, Nikki pounced on her like a wild tiger on its prey. She dragged Karen inside through the kitchen door and threw her to the floor. With Karen on the floor, Nikki climbed on top of her tearing her clothes off with no mercy.

"Stop! Please! I'll give it to you. You can have my fruit." Karen pleaded.

"No Bitch! You too damn tired." Nikki screamed before slapping Karen's face. "Tired from what? Is my fruit spoiled" Did Lance touch my fruit?"

"No!" Karen answered with her hand on her face.

"Do you want Mama to have it or not?" Nikki was smiling.

"Yes Mama." I want you to have it." Karen removed her torn pants and her panties. She spread her legs as her breathing got shallow. She held open the lips of her pussy like Nikki loved for her to do. Nikki always said that was the invitation for her to bite into the fruit. She waited for Nikki to get undressed but instead, Nikki looked at her.

"Let me check out this damn fruit. It needs to be inspected." Nikki looked at Karen and laughed wickedly. She then inserted two fingers inside Karen, hard and forceful. She continued in and out of Karen with more force each time.

"You're hurting me!" Karen tried to close her legs. When she did, Nikki pinched the lips of her pussy.

"Open your damn legs and shut the hell up. You said your damn ass is tired didn't you?" She took her fingers out of Karen and started beating her pussy with the palms of her hand.

"Stop Nikki!"

"Don't you tell me when to stop with your tired ass." Nikki went from using the palms of her hand to using her fists. "I will beat this damn fruit until it is bruised and good for nothing. Do you understand me Bitch? Make that your last damn time telling me that you are too tired for me."

"I'm sorry Mama. Please forgive me." Karen had tears in her eyes. She wanted to be rid of Nikki like yesterday.

"Did you buy that strap-on like I told you to do?"

"Yes Mama, I got it. It's in the room.

"Go get it! Now Bitch." Nikki demanded.

Karen went into her bedroom to get the new strap-on. *I can't take this damn shit. My pussy is already sore as hell from that bitch hitting it. No matter what it takes I have to get her the hell up out of here. This is nothing short of sheer torture.*

"Hurry the hell up. What is taking you so damn long?" Nikki yelled from the other room.

"I have it." Karen answered as she handed the strap-on to Nikki. After Nikki was strapped up, she knocked Karen to the floor.

"Let's at least go to the bedroom and get in the bed." Karen suggested.

"I'm running this damn show. I call the shots. Open your legs and get ready for this big dick." Nikki yelled at her.

Karen did as she was told. Nikki took no mercy on her. "Whose damn fruit is this bitch?"

"It's your fruit. It's yours."

"Does Mama take care of this fruit?"

"Yes!"

Nikki stopped and took Karen's face into her right hand, squeezing her jaws. "You have spoiled it for tonight. I can't even get a damn orgasm. If you spoil it again, I'll kill you."

Karen nodded her head that she understood. Nikki climbed off her and let the strap-on drop to the floor. When Karen stood, Nikki held her in her arms. "Mama loves you when you are being good. Stop upsetting Mama. You know that I just want you to behave so we can have fun. I'm going to take good care of that fruit. Okay?"

"Okay." Karen answered.

Nikki laughed a wicked hysterical laugh. "Oh my precious Boo. If you make me... ha...ha...ha! I mean... if you really make me...ha...ha...ha...! I'll cut that fruit to the damn core...ha...ha...ha! Now get cleaned up!"

Karen prayed on her way to the linen closet. *Lord, I know that I haven't always done the right thing but if you will just help me out of this, I will be so grateful. I promise that I'll do better. Please help me lord. Please don't let me down because if you don't help me, I'm afraid that I'm going to have to kill her.*

Chapter 14

Rhonda walked into the house with Nard and kicked off her shoes. It had been a long stressful day at the Developmental Evaluation Center. Nard had gone through a battery of test, observations and evaluations. Rhonda had refused to believe there was a problem with their son. "The child is just lazy." She had said. "He'll talk when he gets ready. He doesn't have anything to say."

Rhonda couldn't understand Bernard not wanting to accompany her to DEC. Since Bernard worked with exceptional children and always complained about parents being in denial, she was stunned at his attitude. He was the first to say that early intervention was the key.

The doctors used CHAT, a modified checklist for autism in toddlers. CHAT is a questionnaire consisting of forty items. The parents' fill out the first section and the doctor fills out the second section. As Rhonda filled out her section, tears strolled down her face. Why hadn't she noticed the early signs? His lack of speech, his repetitive body movements, his impaired social skills, his limited interest in play and his lack of eye contact were all things she had overlooked. Even when he didn't respond to his name, she thought he was just ignoring her. Now she understood. He wasn't ignoring her at all. He just didn't know.

The doctors also used CARS which is a childhood autism rating scale consisting of five diagnostic domains and fifteen questions. It assesses adaptiveness to change, verbal responses, communication, and relating to others.

Rhonda had sat in DEC feeling helpless and stupid. Helpless because there was nothing she could do and stupid because she had been so caught up in her own problems that she failed to recognize Nard had an even bigger one.

They had a trained psychologist to administer the Bayley Scales test which assesses motor skills, mental agility and behavior. After the battery of test were completed, two doctors and a psychologist joined Rhonda in a room to explain to her that Nard is autistic.

"What can you do to fix this? She had asked. "Is he going to have to be on medication?"

"I'm afraid it can't be fixed Mrs. Simpson." One of the doctors answered her and went on to explain. "Autism is a complex developmental disability that impairs one's social skills as well as their expressive and receptive communication. There is no cure for autism but with early intervention and the proper resources, Bernard can learn to function. I'm sorry. I know this is not the news you were expecting to hear."

Rhonda covered her face with her hands and the feelings she had tried so hard to suppress ran freely as she screamed and cried loudly.

"May I call someone for you?"

"No, I'm fine." She answered.

"Here is a pamphlet for you on autism and here is a list of the most frequently asked questions and the answers to those questions. If I can be of further assistance to you please call our center to speak with me, or any of the other doctors here. I will fax all of this to your son's doctor." The psychologist patted her on the shoulder. The other doctors followed behind him as they left the room. Rhonda had decided she would wait for Bernard to get home to tell him about the diagnosis. There was no need to bother him at work. She watched while Nard sat on the floor with a shoestring swinging it back and forth. He seemed to be fascinated by the string. Rhonda had observed him doing this before but she had brushed it off. *How could I not have known there was a problem? Oh my goodness.*

The key turned in the door and startled Rhonda. Bernard was not expected home for another couple of hours. *I guess he thought about it and was anxious to hear what the doctors had to say.* The thought Rhonda had in her head quickly diminished as soon as she saw the expression on his face, Bernard looked pale and it was as if he had aged seven years since she saw him before he left for his job.

"What's up Baby? What's wrong?" She asked.

"Have you seen the news? You don't even have the television on!" His voice trembled as he spoke in a loud tone.

"You are starting to scare me. Tell me what the hell is going on Bernard." She demanded.

He ignored Nard on the floor and walked right past him to where Rhonda was standing. Taking her by the hand, he led her to the couch where they both had a seat. "Baby please don't be alarmed. Everything is going to be fine. The police came to my job because no one was here when they came by the house."

"Police! What did the police want? What is going on?"

"Its Nikki. She has wandered off from Brooksville."

"What?" She shouted. "Wandered off? There is no such a damn thing as she wandered off. You don't just wander off from a mental institution where crazy ass people are locked in."

"Who knows Baby? Maybe she stole keys from one of the orderlies. Nikki can be very clever when she wants to be and if she wants something bad enough." He squeezed Rhonda's hand.

She was quiet; lost in thought as her mind drifted back to her visit at Brooksville. *Damn! That sorry ass motherfucka. Nikki didn't steal any keys. It was that orderly. She has something on him. I'm sure of it. The way he let her handle me and didn't raise a hand to stop her. Fuck him. I know he's behind this shit. I'd bet my life on it.*

"Sweetheart, are you listening to me?"

Rhonda shook her head. "Yes Bernard. I'm listening. It just doesn't make sense."

He stood and walked to the bar. "I need a drink. Would you like one?" He asked Rhonda.

"Nah! I'm fine." She answered.

"You are not fine Rhonda and that's understandable but I don't want you to worry. They are going to catch her and put her back where she belongs. The police said she'd be crazy to come this way." Bernard downed his drink with one gulp.

"Say what?" Rhonda looked at him. "She'd be crazy to come here huh? Why the fuck do they think she was locked in a damn mental institution? Because she has good sense? This is just too much. I can't deal with this mess right now. Dean will be home soon and we haven't talked about what the doctors said." She stood. "I think I will have that drink after all. Anything you fix will be fine."

Rhonda explained to him that Bernard had autism. After hearing about the tests and the results, he could no longer deny there was a problem. "Baby, I just didn't do what I was suppose to do. There is no way I shouldn't have known there was a problem. Maybe I just didn't want to see it. One in every 150 boys is born autistic. Why Nard? Do you think I am being punished for getting involved with Nikki? Maybe this is the Lord's way of paying me back."

Honey, you can't blame yourself for this. The doctors told me that nobody knows what causes autism, but now that we know, we can take the appropriate steps to help him. We'll get through this."

Chapter 15

It had only been a few days since Shemeka moved to Florida but Brandi missed her already. She knew that Meka had really gone through hell trying to cope with the loss of Robert. Even though he turned out to be a female who was born Roberta, they all continued to refer to him as Robert. She didn't know how she was going to manage without having her friend there for the late night talks and advice so it was good that she had Anthony back in her life. Brandi wondered what Meka would say if she knew about her seeing Anthony again. *Probably have a damn fit.* She turned on Anthony's street.

Brandi approached his house just in time to see him walking Jessica to her car. She drove pass the house and parked in the next block. Glancing in her rear view mirror she could see Anthony kiss Jessica before opening the car door and helping her in. *Damn! I wonder if he fucked her. I am having a hard time with this bullshit. I don't give a damn if she did stick by him. I wonder how long she'd stick around if she knew I was getting the dick. Maybe I should find a way to let her know.*

Brandi waited a few minutes before driving around the block. She got out of her car and walked up to the house. She hesitated before ringing the doorbell. *I wonder if he fucked her. He's not going to be able to have both of us.* She rang the doorbell.

"Who da hell is it?" Anthony asked.

"Who the hell do you want it to be?" Brandi still loved him in spite of everything. He didn't do her wrong. She was the one who had not stood by him. She had made a mistake and now she needed to correct that mistake. Anthony opened the door wearing shorts and a tee shirt. He looked so sexy.

"Hey Baybee. Check dis out. Why da hell ya pop up ova here witout callin first? Don do dat shit no mo. Ya don no wat I might have goin on. Understan?

Brandi was hurt and disappointed that he would talk to her like that. "I thought you would be glad to see me. Apparently not. Do you want me to leave?"

"Don't be silly gurl. I'm glad ta see ya but just don do dat shit no mo. It's such a thang as respeck."

Brandi didn't respond.

"Come on in and make yaself at home. I been working out. Ima take a quick shower and den Ima be rite with ya.." He kissed Brandi on the forehead before heading to the bathroom. "Go on in da bedroom. I won be long." He yelled back

Brandi went to the bedroom and undressed. She usually kept a night-tee in her bag but left it on the coffee table when she rushed out of the house in such a hurry to get to Anthony. It was no problem though because he'd rather see her nakedness. She folded her clothes neatly and placed them on the nightstand. As she looked to the left of the nightstand she observed a nine-millimeter pistol of some sort on the dresser. Her nerves started to race. *What the fuck? Isn't this fool on probation? What the hell is he thinking?*

Anthony entered the bedroom with a towel wrapped around his waist. "Ready or not, here I come." He laughed.

"Honey, what in the hell are you doing with a gun?" She questioned. "You know that I don't like guns, and you know that you are not suppose to have weapons. Can't they lock you back up for that?"

"Don start Brandi. Ya no I'm drivin a truck and ya know how crazy people is nowadays. Plus, somebody threaten me. I don no who it is. Dey called from a private number. Ya no how niggas get jealous and don wanna see ya doin good. I thin dey be drinkin dat haterade. I'm not worrin bout it but I'm not getting caught out der witout my shit neither.

Brandi tried to relax but she felt somewhat nervous. Surely Anthony wouldn't be stupid enough to get back in the game. But maybe he was. She remembered that Redd had been to his house the other day. She no longer felt comfortable being there without knowing what was going on.

"Anthony, I completely forgot about Rhonda. She invited me to come over this evening and share some things with her and Bernard on autism. They recently found out that Nard is autistic and they are going through it right about now. I need to go to them. I don't want to let them down." She gathered her clothes from the nightstand. Anthony knew she was using Nard's situation as an excuse to leave.

"Go da fuck on den. I dint invite ya ass ova here in da first damn place.

Brandi quickly put her clothes on and left without a word to Anthony. *What the hell is going on?* She drove down the busy street with more questions than answers. *Can he be stupid enough to jeopardize his freedom? Am I over exaggerating? Are people that damn jealous of him that someone would try to kill his ass? Maybe I am not being as supportive as I should be. I know that people will hate on you when you are doing well. He's done his time. He was punished for his crime. It wouldn't be fair to keep making him pay. I should turn around and go back but not now. This is not the time. He's upset with me right now. I'll wait til tomorrow. I was wrong. I will make it up to him.* Brandi decided to go home.

****

Anthony paced around the room. It was a relief that Brandi had gone. He cared about her but he didn't want to see her hurt. She probably suspected that he was dealing again. Life was hard. How in the hell did she think he was going to make it in the world? Oh yeah. Logan Transit. The job paid decent but he didn't want to drive a truck until he was an old ass man. Once he made enough money and got some of the things he wanted, he was going to quit anyway. That's how he had gotten caught the first time. He was greedy and didn't have the good sense to quit while he was ahead. Besides; this drug thing was bigger than him. He only scratched the damn surface. How does a black man fresh out of prison get his hands on drugs and money like that? He doesn't. Not unless he has a rich person backing him. Anthony didn't like the idea of having a partner. He was a solo operator. The last partner he had dealt with rolled over on him and made a deal with the Feds.

This time was different. His partner was cool and his partner had more to lose than he did. At first Anthony was skeptical thinking it could possibly have been a set up. Why would this person befriend him and want to help him get back on his feet? After about four weeks of getting to know this person, Anthony began to feel more comfortable and relaxed. No undercover cop would go the lengths his partner had gone.

Anthony's phone chirped, signaling that he had received a text message. He looked at the phone and pressed view. *I'm sorry Anthony. Please give me a chance to make it right.* Anthony pressed 'reply'. *How can ya make it rite wen ya wit anuther man? I don roll like dat. Ima be ya only man or not ya man at all. Datz just da way it tis.* He knew that he was being a hypocrite. He was messing around with Brandi and he had Jessica. He had sexed people he met on his truck runs, but that was a little different. It was the nature of the beast. Plus, he never got caught.

Wasn't it ok to cheat if you never got caught? Wasn't it about respect and keeping the shit so far away that your partner never found out about it? But damn! When you consider someone your damn soul-mate, a person you would die for, and you catch that person in bed with another man, wouldn't that shit tear anybody apart? That was worse than when the judge gave him all that time.

Although Jessica had been there with him when he got out, she wasn't his soul mate. He felt a sense of obligation to her but she would never have his heart. All she could have was the Woodruff name. In a way, he regretted deceiving her but she was the one who insisted on a ring and fabulous wedding. He felt like he owed her that much. No need in hurting her.

His cell phone chirped again. He looked at the reply. *How many times do I have to apologize? I was wrong. I just got weak and one thing led to another. Please forgive me. We have gone through too much to throw it away like that over a damn man who I don't even want. You are the one I want. I want to love you. Please say you'll forgive me.*

Anthony texted back, *Ya hurt me bad. Ya didn't hafta do me like dat. I hav mo den enuff dick to satisfy ya. Do ya even understan how bad dat shit hurt me? I can't give ya a anzer rite now. I'll let ya know.* Anthony turned his phone off and went to his weight room. *Dis some stressful ass shit. I need me a gud workout.*

Chapter 16

Nikki sat curled up on the couch watching *A Time to Kill.* She had watched that movie numerous of times and her reaction was always the same. *Sick ass muthafuckas!! Raping a damn child. Putting their nasty ass sperm in her precious little body. Any fool should know that is justification to kill a bastard. There is nothing I hate worse than a motherfucka who puts his nasty ass dick in an innocent child. Somebody should cut the muthafuckas dick off and shove it in his mouth before shooting him in the got damn head!!!* Nikki screamed as if someone were actually in the room with her listening to every word she said.

She sprang to her feet when she heard the doorbell. From behind the curtain she could see Lance's car in the driveway. "Just a minute." She yelled as she ran to the door. "Hey Baby. Come on in."

Lance came into the house and kissed Nikki. She put her arms around him and welcomed him with a nice wet and juicy tongue kiss. His manhood immediately started to rise.

"Here. I brought you something." He handed Nikki a bag. "Lunch. I know how much you like Chinese. I thought we'd have lunch together. Sweet and sour chicken for me, and sweet and sour shrimp for you."

She took the bag. "Thanks Lance. You are so thoughtful. Let's eat and then I will show you how much I appreciate you." Nikki put the food on the table and winked at Lance. "I've been wondering how long it would be before you brought this dick to me. Umph! I've been wondering about having your fat rod up in me."

Lance smiled. "I've been thinking about you too. I just had to be careful. They've been investigating and everybody is trying to figure out how you could have escaped. They checked for all the ID badges because that is the only way to swipe you out. Apparently Ms. Covington dropped her badge on the floor when she left in such a hurry to get to the hospital. The thing they are trying to figure out now is how you got out of your room, which should have been locked. The chief investigator thinks that someone accidentally left your room unlocked. I don't think anyone suspects that you were aided in your escape. Thank goodness."

"Well it's good that nobody suspects you Sexy. I think that we are going to be just fine. I appreciate everything you have done for me. After lunch you will see. I will show you." Nikki smiled at him. She knew that the key to Lance was to pacify him. If she pacified him, she could get him to do just about anything. After all, the fool had risked his job and his freedom to help her escape.

"Good Sweetheart. You know how much I miss having those lips wrapped around my dick." He laughed out loud.

Stupid ass bastard. Nikki thought as she smiled at him. *You make me sick to my damn stomach.* Nikki continued to eat her sweet and sour shrimp. In between bites she'd glance at Lance and flash him a seductive look. "Lance. That was great but I am full. Let's take this to the bedroom."

Lance jumped up like a jack-n-the-box. "Lead the way."

Once they were in the bedroom, Nikki unzipped his pants. His nine-inch dick was full and erect. He smiled as Nikki took all of him in and out of her mouth. "Ah Baby! Oh that feels so good Nikki. Damn woman! You sho-nuff know how to suck a dick. Yeeees," Lance started to feel weak in the knees as he held on to Nikki's head. "Damn, this feels good. Lay down. I want to feel my dick in that hot pussy of yours."

Nikki moved from the floor to the bed. *Shit* She thought. *I hate that shit. At least his rabbit ass won't take that long and I can get down to business.*

Lance put his hard dick into Nikki. He pounded her pussy hard and fast like a driver in the Daytona 500. Nikki knew that the more she talked to his jack rabbit ass, the quicker he would be done.

"Ah yeah. Fuck me Baby. Give me this dick."

The more she talked the more confident he felt. "You like this damn dick don't you? This feels good to that pussy don't it?"

"I love your dick. You make my pussy feel great. Ah…damn! Oh Lance. Oh…that's so damn good Baby. It is …gooo…oo.ood!"

"Nikki, I'm about… to …blow…Oh…Oh…ohhhhhhhh…shit!"

"Me too…go ahead. Give it to me. Fuck me. That's it. Oh yeah!"

"Ahhh..oooooh! Yessss. Me…too. Ahhhh!" Lance pressed hard into her as if he wanted her to have every single drop of his juices. He climbed down and fell back on the bed next to her. "Damn that was good. Nikki I love you. You've got the best damn pussy I ever had."

Where the fuck did that love shit come from? Nikki asked herself. "I know you do Lance." She answered. She moved closer to him and let her head rest on his chest. "Lance, I need a favor. It's very important to me."

"Anything. Name it. What do you need?"

"It's been a long time since I've seen my children. Don't panic. I can feel you tensing up. I don't want you to kidnap them or anything. I just want to get a look at them."

"Ok. Do you want me to get you some pictures?" He questioned.

"No Lance. I wouldn't have you take a chance like that. All I want you to do is find out what schools they attend. I will catch a glance at them without anyone knowing." She looked at Lance. "I'll give you all the information."

"That's fine." He rubbed his hands over Nikki's hair. It was the second time she had ever mentioned her kids to him. He knew that Nikki must be hurting. Anything he could do to aid her in the healing process would be his pleasure. Nikki had shown him how to love. He went to bed each night with her on his mind and woke up each morning with her on his mind. It had gotten to the point that he no longer desired his wife. He'd do anything to prove his love to Nikki. As soon as he was able to afford it, he would find them a nice cottage out in the country where no one would bother them.

"Lance, there is one more thing." Nikki sat straight up in bed. "I also need a gun."

"A gun?" Lance sprang up in bed beside her. "What? Why the fuck do you need a damn gun? I can't get a gun. I don't even like guns!" Lance knew enough about Nikki to know that he didn't want to put a gun in her hands. She could be dangerous. Wasn't her ass in Brooksville because she had killed someone? He loved her but he wasn't feeling that gun shit at all.

"I'm sorry Nikki. I can find out about your kids for you, but I can't do the gun thing. That is out of the question. Don't be mad Baby." He pleaded.

"I'm not mad Baby. I feel you. It's all good." Nikki got out of bed and kissed him. "I have to use the bathroom Boo. Make yourself comfortable. Are you good for a second round?" She asked as she headed out of the room.

Damn. She's more understanding than I thought she'd be. She's wonderful and I'm lucky to have her in my life. Damn the issues. She is a real woman and she's mine. He rubbed his manhood. *Let me get you right for the next go around.* As he thought about how lucky he was to have Nikki in his life, she returned to the bed and kissed him.

"Baby, I was thinking." She told him as she rubbed her hand across his chest. "We seldom have any foreplay any more. We always jump right into making love. And we never ever have after sex." She kissed his chest. "I love being with you." She continued to kiss his body.

"Damn Baby. You are going to make me have to have that second round right now if you keep rubbing and kissing on me like this. My shit is rising already."

Nikki kissed the head of his semi-hard rod. She licked it up and down before squeezing it. She squeezed it harder and harder.

"Whoa! Ease up on a brother. You're hurting me." He grimaced.

"Oops. I'm sorry." She loosened her grip on him and just as his breathing relaxed she squeezed again. She squeezed him hard and held him tight as she grabbed the butcher knife she had eased into the bedroom. When she pressed the knife against his manhood, it immediately crawled into its skin like a turtle retreating to its shell.

"Ni…Ni…Nic…Key. Whhhh..at are you do…ing?" Lance froze. He was scared to move with the knife in Nikki's hand and pressed against his manhood. He didn't want to make her angry.

"I'm trying to decide if I'm going to let you keep this motherfucka or if I'm going to cut it off. I'm trying to decide how the fuck you would look dickless." She growled at him.

"I wouldn't look good dickless Baby. What's wrong Sweetheart? Why do you have a knife? Damn Baby. Please, just tell me what's going on."

"Shut the fuck up Bitch!" Nikki yelled while she pressed the knife closer. "You don't love me. You don't know how to love me. Do I ask your motherfuckin ass for much? Do I? Answer me!"

Lance shook his head no.

"I know damn well that I don't. But I ask you to get me a got damn gun and you freak the hell out. Do you know who I am muthafucka? I will cut your ass from A to Z and use your blood on my hamburger for ketchup. Do you understand?"

"Yeah! Yeah Nikki. I'll get the gun for you. Give me a couple of days. Please don't hurt Mr. Johnson."

Nikki let go of Mr. Johnson and almost laughed in Lance's face. He had the nerve to give that damn thing a name. She let the knife drop to the floor "I don't want to hurt you. Please don't make me hurt you. It seems like you are trying to spoil things. Why you want to do that Baby. Please don't. I don't like it when a man tries to spoil things." She kissed him "I need for you to be obedient."

Lance placed his hand on Mr. Johnson. "I'm going to obey. I'm going to help you. Let me get dressed and get out of here before Karen gets home." He put his clothes on without bothering to shower. As he walked towards the door, Nikki called out to him. "What is it?" He asked.

"Are you going to leave without giving me a kiss?"

"Oh yeah. I wasn't thinking. I was concentrating on getting out of here before Karen walks in the door. I know it is about time for her to get here." He walked back to Nikki and kissed her on the lip.

"You can do better than that can't you?" She teased.

Lance held her head and put his tongue in her mouth. Nikki bit down hard on his tongue.

"Ouch! What the hell you do that for?"

"Just a little reminder before you leave. Don't fuckin cross me." Nikki threatened.

"I won't Nikki."

"I believe you Baby. In that case give Mama a real kiss." Nikki licked her lips.

Shit! Lance thought. *She might bite the whole damn thing off the next time. Or is this a test to see how well I obey?* He was scared not to kiss her. After a brief hesitation, Lance put his tongue in Nikki's mouth and she gave him a passionate kiss.

"I'm sorry Lance. You're trembling. I didn't mean to scare you. I know that I get carried away at times but I don't like it when you make me act ugly. You know that you're my Boo." She kissed him again. "So exactly when will you be back?"

"Give me two days. I'll be seeing you."

Lance breathed a strong sigh of relief when he got in his car. *Whew. That damn woman is crazy for real. And to think, that I considered giving up my wife for her. If it's the last thing I do in this world, I am going to have to find a way to wean myself from her. I hope like hell that Karen knows what she is living with.*

Chapter 17

It had been approximately a week and a half since Nard was diagnosed as being autistic. Bernard was no longer in denial. He accepted the fact that his son was autistic and started going through the proper channels to get him help. Being a certified teacher for exceptional children, he was well aware that early intervention was the key. He arranged for Nard to get speech therapy. A lady came from an agency called Speakability. She came to the Daycare to work with Nard three days a week for forty-five minute sessions. An occupational therapist came twice a week to work with him in thirty-minute sessions. This was to help with his fine and gross motors skills.

Rhonda didn't seem to understand. In her opinion, Nard was fragile.

"We can't do this shit unless we work together. You are not helping him with all this pity party bullshit. Damn."

"Bernard it's going to take time. He's just a child. He doesn't know." Rhonda felt protective of Nard.

"I understand that he doesn't know. That's why it's up to us to teach him." Bernard walked to the kitchen with Dean following close behind.

"Daddy can I have some ice cream?" She asked in a soft voice.

"I guess I can manage that. Would you like to top it off with some cookies?"

She smiled at him. "Yeah! That sounds good."

Nard walked into the kitchen and saw the cookies on the counter. "Ugh…ugh…ugh!" He pointed to the cookies.

Dean looked at him. "Oh! Do you want some cookies? We forgot all about you in there playing." She picked up the box and stuck her hand in to get him a cookie.

"No! Don't give him any cookies. Make him ask for them."

Rhonda heard the conversation and rushed into the kitchen. "How is he going to ask when he doesn't know how Bernard? Pointing is what he does. That is how he communicates his wants for right now."

"Stop it Rhonda. He has to at least try." Bernard scolded.

Dean looked confused. She didn't want to be in the middle of whatever was going on. "I'm going to go back in here and watch Dora the Explorer." She walked out of the kitchen with her ice cream and cookies. Bernard was fixated on the box and continued to point.

Bernard put his son's hand down. "Stop pointing. What do you want? Those are cookies. Say cook…ies. You can say it. Coo.ok…ies."

Nard started squirming and it was apparent to Rhonda that he was getting agitated. Rhonda picked him up and held him in her arms. She took two chocolate chip cookies from the box. "Let him have the damn box and stop torturing him." She told her husband before giving Nard the cookies.

"Rhonda, I'm sick of this shit. You are not helping the situation at all. We won't always be around to hand him things. He needs to learn to communicate. It will benefit him to learn how to express himself. He may not do it perfect but we need to help him understand how to do this to the best of his ability and that's not it."

"Well I just hate to see him like that. Imagine how frustrated you would be if you were trying to tell somebody something and they didn't understand you or what you wanted."

Bernard threw his hands in the air. "How can we possibly help him if we are pulling in two different directions? It is almost like fighting a losing battle. We are going to have to be on one accord or Nard is going to be the one who slips through the cracks. Damn! You just don't get it do you?" He picked up his keys from the hall table. "I've got to get out of here before I say the wrong thing."

****

Nikki felt good staking out Bernard's house. She wanted to be close to Rhonda. For some reason, Rhonda just didn't understand that they were soul mates. She was about to cut her car lights off when Bernard came flying out of the garage. Nikki knew that speed all too well. It was the *My wife pissed me the fuck off* speed. Nikki had planned to camp out all night and wait for the perfect chance to get with Rhonda but this might be even better. From the way he was driving she knew she wouldn't be able to catch up with him but she didn't have to. Old habits die hard. She knew exactly where he was headed. To the bar.

She waited in the car about half an hour to give him time to get a little tipsy. He was a creature of habit. The first time she had met him, it was at the same bar. He had downed one too many drinks and she pretended to be drunk herself. After he had taken her home, she seduced him.

Nikki walked into the bar and spotted Bernard on the stool gulping down a drink. She sat at a table and waited for someone to take her drink order. The wig that Karen had purchased for her, along with the reading glasses came in handy. Lance was going to have to do better. Even though he managed to come through with a gun, that lil measly ass $70.00 was not getting it. *He must have lost his fuckin mind.* Nikki thought. *What the hell is wrong with these damn men? Why in the hell do they think a woman is supposed to give them good pussy for a handful of crumbs? That doesn't make any damn sense to me. If the truth be told, I can make myself holla louder than any man ever made me holla. Real talk! Besides that, when a woman gives a stupid ass man her body, she is giving him the best thing she can possibly give him.*

Nikki's thoughts were interrupted when the cocktail waitress came to get her drink order. "Let me have Crown and coke. Oh yeah. And how about giving the gentleman at the bar with the blue shirt on, another round of whatever he is drinking.

"Sure thing. I'll be back in a few." The waitress hurried off.

Bernard looked in Nikki's direction. It was clear that he didn't recognize her. He held the drink up and nodded his head to thank her. He turned the drink up without stopping. When he stepped off the bar stool, he staggered.

Damn! Nikki laughed. *Damn wimp never could hold his liquor.*

Bernard patted his pockets, feeling for his keys. He was barely able to stand when the bar tender noticed him "Hey Buddy. Why don't you have a seat? I'll call a taxi for you. You are in no shape to drive. If I let you leave here like that and something happens, I could be held liable." He helped Bernard to a chair at one of the tables.

"I've only had one drink. I'll take him home and then come back for my car. I've known him for a while. We go way back." Nikki took Bernard's keys, which the bartender had confiscated. "Lean on me Buddy." She told him.

Once Bernard was at his car, Nikki took his wallet out of his pants before helping him in. Then she climbed in the driver's seat. "Now where do I take your ass?"

Bernard leaned back in the passenger's seat with his head against the door. "You're pretty." He told Nikki. "You remind me of somebody."

"Yeah, I know." She answered as she continued to drive. Nikki decided on the Super 8 since it was back off the highway and very little traffic flowed that way. When she pulled into the parking lot she got out and checked in. She paid for the room with the money from Bernard's wallet. After getting the room key, she returned to the car to find Bernard asleep. "Wake up!"

"Ah…yeah…yeah…I'm woke."

Nikki helped him out of the car and to the room. "What's going on?" Bernard questioned.

"Nothing but pussy Baby. Nothing but sweet pussy." Nikki snickered.

"Pussy? Okay. Yeah. I want some pussy."

Nikki lay Bernard on the bed and undressed him. Before putting his wallet back in his pants, she removed a hundred dollar from it.

Bernard opened his eyes when he felt her hand on his magic stick. She licked up and down the side of his stick while massaging it. Do you want me to put this bad boy in my mouth?" She asked him speaking a little bit above a whisper.

"Yes." He managed to say. Bernard could feel his magic stick coming to life. "Yes! Suck my dick. Come on now, what you waiting on. Suck this thang." He begged.

Nikki licked the head of Bernard's stick. She licked it all over and worked his shaft while he moaned. When she took his magic stick in her mouth, he got louder.

"Um…oh…yeah…that feels so damn good to me."

When she felt him tensing up, she stopped.

"No! Hell no. Don't stop lady." He pleaded.

Nikki ignored him and got undressed. While Bernard rubbed his hands up and down his magic stick. She knew he was ready to release himself. *Rhonda probably hasn't given him any. She knows that damn cookie belongs to me.* With a faint whisper in his ear, she asked, "Do you want to fuck me?"

"Oh my goodness yeah. You know I want to fuck you. What man wouldn't want to go up in you? Let me fuck you."

"Just lay there and enjoy the ride." Nikki climbed on top of Bernard.

He lay stretched out on the bed in the dimly lit room. He didn't know who was riding him like a cowgirl and he didn't care. It felt good to be with a woman who enjoyed and appreciated his magic stick. Rhonda was always tired and acting like she didn't want it. Well tonight somebody wanted it and she was making him feel like a real man.

"Umph...go ahead Lady. Ride that dick. This pussy is hot as hell." He told her. "Oh yes."

She rubbed his chest. "Yes... give me this dick. Fuck me." As she continued to ride Bernard, she noticed that he was getting into his zone. She slowed down to a nice pace.

"Tell me it's good."

"It's good." Bernard tightened his grip on her thighs. Nikki climbed down.

"NO! Don't stop. I was almost there. Why did you stop?"

Bernard was on edge. He was ready to come. "Please! Give me that good pussy."

Nikki took her wig and glasses off before flipping on the lamp. Bernard sat straight up in bed. "Oh no! Nikki what the hell you doing?"

"Shhh...we'll talk later."

She held his magic stick in her hand and licked it. "Do you want this pussy? Do you want to fuck me?"

"Yes Nikki. I want it." Bernard could not deny that Nikki made him feel great. His magic stick was hard and he wanted to release it. Nikki sucked him hard.

"I've missed you. Umph! Fuck me Bernard." Nikki lay on the bed beside him. Bernard tried to stand up but he was unable to stand alone without stumbling. He wanted to put his magic stick deep inside her wetness and stroke her but he couldn't. Nikki had the juiciest pussy he ever stuck his stick into.

"Get back on top Nikki. Please. Ride this thang Baby."

Nikki climbed back on Bernard. She rode him slowly at first and then she increased her speed. Within five minutes he was clutching her thighs and trembling.

"Augh! Damn!" He screamed. "Whew!

Nikki was satisfied. It didn't matter that she hadn't cum. As long as Bernard got his, as long as she knew she could still get to him.

"Damn you Nikki." He said in a whisper. "What the hell are you doing here any way? Stay the hell away from my family and me and I mean it."

"Muthafucka, that's not what you said a minute ago when you were begging for my pussy. I'll stay away from you. I haven't seen you and you haven't seen me. As soon as I shower and get dressed, I'm out of here. I'll catch a taxi back." She threw his keys on the bed. "Remember Sweetheart." She blew him a kiss. "We haven't seen each other."

Bernard hung his head. He had messed up. Once again, he had put his magic stick where it did not belong. Rhonda could never find out about this. Never. "Nikki we haven't seen each other. Please hurry with your shower and leave." He buried his face in the pillow.

Chapter 18

Anthony looked at the caller ID of his ringing cell phone. *Number withheld.* "Why da hell do ya keep doin dat? Ya no I don like ta anzer dem calls from numbers when I don no who is callin. Wat up?" He waited for an answer. Redd had gotten back with the merchandise about an hour ago. "Everythin is straight." He continued to listen. "Yeah Sexy but I'm da one takin all da risk. Nobody no bout ya and I wudn't let none of dis touch ya. I don have nunthin but bout nine street dealers and Redd handles dem and distributes ta dem. Even Redd don't know who ya are."

Anthony walked to the bar to fix himself a drink. "Sexy ya worry too much. Pleeze don brin dat mess with ya ta da cabin dis weekend. It's gon be all bout us. Thanks Honey. It's gon be all bout us. I love ya. Bye."

When Anthony hung up the telephone he laughed out loud. *Damn! Ain't nobody wud believ me if I told it. Wudn't nobody believe I'm dickin da hell out ya sexy ass. Ya mite hav da coke connect but I got da gud dick and dat trumps anythin else.* Anthony prided himself on always satisfying his partner. *It's not my fault dat ya damn man couldn't satisfy ya fine sexy ass. When ya run upon sum gud dick, wat else are ya pose ta do?*

Anthony was feeling confident and full of life. His telephone rang again and he recognized Brandi's number. "Wat up Brandi? Oh! Ya in da nayborhud huh? Yeah its fine ta stop by. Sure. See ya in five minutes."

When Brandi arrived she was apologetic. "Sorry about the other night Anthony. I don't know what got into me. I guess I was just nervous. Guns make me uneasy. I realize that you have to have protection."

"Thanks Ba fer understandin. It's fucked up out here. People don wanna see ya hav nunthin. I work too hard fer my shit ta let sum lowlife break in here and take it."

Brandi understood. She loved Anthony. Deep down he was a great person. Why was she the only one who seemed to realize that? She remembered the strange look on Rhonda's face two days ago when she confessed that she had started back kicking it with Anthony. For some reason beyond her knowledge, Rhonda had gotten very upset with her. It had almost turned into an argument.

"Why would you go back to that after you have gotten away from it?" Rhonda had asked. "Is good dick that important to you or do you just have such low self esteem that you don't care?"

"I have excellent self esteem!" Brandi had fired back at her. "And how would you know the dick is good? You never had any."

"Girl please! He's a damn man. He doesn't have any loyalties to you or anyone else. Do you actually think that if his dick got hard he wouldn't fuck me?"

"That's my point Rhonda. His dick wouldn't even get hard for you. Bernard's barely gets there."

Brandi knew she had said too much when she recognized the hurt look on her friends face. "I'm sorry Rhonda. Please forgive me. I never should have said that. I'm just frustrated. There is so much going on in my head."

"It's okay." Rhonda responded. "Don't worry about it. Bernard does have problems at times. But you best trust and believe that Anthony's dick would get hard as hell for a sexy ass woman like me. I'm going to have to catch you later. Nard has an appointment."

Brandi felt bad. All Rhonda was doing was trying to look out for her. Shemeka was gone and Rhonda was only trying to make sure she didn't get in so deep with Anthony that she ended up getting hurt. Now she was at Anthony's with the desire to prove Rhonda wrong. Anthony would never even look at her friend twice. He wouldn't hurt her like that.

"Baby would you like for me to fix you a drink?" He asked Brandi.

"Sure. You know how I like it." She answered.

Anthony fixed two drinks. He gave Brandi her drink in one hand and took her by the other hand to lead her to the bedroom. He hit a switch on the wall and music began to play. They swayed to the music for a minute before Anthony sat on the bench at the foot of his bed. "Hav a seat Ba and tell me wat goin on with ya."

"Nothing is going on. I'm good. I had you on my mind and I wanted to spend some time with you." She answered.

"Well dat's all…rite." Anthony dragged the words out not quite knowing what to tell her. He knew that Brandi expected him to throw some dick up in her but he had to get packed for his weekend escapade and he needed to preserve all of his energy for that. It was going to be a long drive up to the cabin tomorrow but it was well worth the drive. Just to be free and relaxed and not have to worry about hiding was going to be awesome.

"Brandi, I don wan ya ta be upset but I gotta get me sum rest. I got a pretty long run in da morning and I'm pooped out."

"No Baby. I understand. It's all good. I just wanted to spend some time with you."

Anthony got up and moved to the bed. He fluffed the pillows on the bed before lying across the bed. "Come here and lay in my arms fer a minute. Ya know we don hav ta hav sex eva time ya come ova."

Brandi smiled. She didn't care what Rhonda or anybody else said about Anthony. He had done his time, paid his debt, and was ready to be reintegrated into society and into her life. "Baby, that's one of the reasons I love you so much. It's not just about sex with us. We are friends. We communicate. You are my soul mate. I can talk to you about anything. I have never been so in tuned with a man before. I love you." She squeezed her arm across his chest as he lay there thinking.

"I know ya do Brandi. I know ya love me." He replied.

Brandi noticed that Anthony had not come back with *I love you too.* She wondered. *Does he not love me any more? Did I hurt him so badly when I turned my back on him that he can't forgive me and get past it? Maybe he just has other things on his mind. He does have that long run tomorrow.*

He interrupted her thoughts. "Ya hungrie? Let's order sum grub. Whatcha got a taste fer?"

"Let's do something simple." Brandi sat up in bed. "How about some hot wings and fries with ranch on the side?"

Anthony retrieved his cell phone from the nightstand. "Sounds gud ta me." He glanced at Brandi before calling in the order. *Ya'd hate me fereva if ya new how I wuz spendin my weekend.* He thought.

Chapter 19

Rhonda got up and got ready for her weekend getaway. Her bags were already packed. She was ready to put some distance between herself and Bernard. He didn't seem to understand. For some reason, he wanted to push Nard and the boy was not ready. She loved Nard as if he was her own son. In fact, he was her son. She was the only mother he had ever known. Giving birth to a child didn't make you a mother by any stretch of the imagination.

Rhonda was just tripping. Nards autism wasn't the sole purpose of her getting away for the weekend. Bernard couldn't always satisfy her and the shit was getting old. Sometimes he would realize he hadn't done anything for her and he would eat her sweetness. But what about the times when he thought he had handled his business and he would roll over and go to sleep.

What about a few nights ago when she was sleep? Rhonda had been awakened from Bernard rubbing her body with his left hand. When she opened her eyes, she could see in the dimly lit room that he was rubbing his semi-hard magic stick. He kept rubbing her until he touched the hairs on her sweetness. When he inserted a finger in her, she began to get aroused. "Umph!" She managed to mumble.

"Baby, I didn't mean to wake you." He whispered. "This stick is wanting to cum in your sweetness real bad."

"I want it too Baby. My sweetness is moist."

Bernard removed the sheet that partially covered her body. After he spread her legs, he inserted his magic stick into her sweetness. Although it wasn't bone hard, it went in.

"Ah! This feels good. Um…Rhonda…Damn!"

Rhonda lay there wet and almost motionless. She hoped that her lack of movement would make Bernard last long enough for her to get her climax.

"Let me put these legs over my shoulder." He suggested. When he lifted her legs, his semi-hard magic stick kept slipping out. "Wait. Turn around. We are going to do your favorite position."

Rhonda livened up. She loved to be fucked doggie style. She got on her hands and knees and Bernard finally got his stick in. It felt good. "Oh yeees!" She said as he held her around the waist and stroked.

But in three minutes he was gripping her waist tighter, and pressing himself hard into her. He gave out a loud, "Oooooh! Tha…at's it Bay…beee!" And then he was finished.

Rhonda tried her best to hide her disappointment. Maybe it was her fault. Maybe they should have had better communication. Maybe she should have explained to him that he wasn't doing enough to get her to where she needed to be. What the hell was wrong with him any way? Didn't he know any damn thing about foreplay? Whatever happened to the kissing, caressing, sucking breast, and tasting the sweetness? Didn't she deserve that? Why did it always have to be about him? What about her?

At least with crazy ass Nikki, she made sure to handle her business. She would never stop unless she was sure that Rhonda was satisfied. Not once had Nikki left her hanging.

But Bernard...nah! He was a selfish ass bastard who only thought of self gratification. As long as he got his shit off, he was pleased. He didn't even taste her sweetness. His ass thought he had done something because he had given it to her in her favorite position. Shortly after he spilled his juices in her, he was fast asleep.

Rhonda didn't bother to get up and go to her toy drawer in the bathroom. She was disappointed but she needed to finish. She touched her sweetness. She stuck her finger in her wetness. It felt good. Her clitoris was begging for attention. She touched it. "Um...umph!" She moaned softly. Rhonda played with herself until her body gave in to the pleasure she had sought from her husband.

While he slept soundly on his side of the bed, her side of the bed had shaken as if it was in an earthquake. Rhonda tipped out of bed to bathe. Bernard was clueless that she had handled her business without him.

Now that Rhonda was getting ready for her weekend trip, she was elated. She had never thought she'd be going on a trip without Bernard and the kids but it was not about them this weekend. It was about her. No matter how bad it seemed or how wrong it seemed, she had to have this weekend.

Rhonda laid out all the clothes the kids would need. Bernard sat up in bed.

"Hi Baby. I have everything you will need for the kids right here on the dresser. I already have spaghetti cooked for when they get out of school today. Just take it out of the fridge and warm it up. Throw some salad mix on their plate. Nard will only eat French dressing and Dean will eat any kind except Italian. Remember that Nard hates tomatoes and Dean won't eat her salad without croutons. Kool-aid is also in the fridge. Rhonda tried to remember if there was anything else Bernard needed to know.

"Oh yeah. You know that tomorrow is Saturday. It's our day to eat out at McDonalds and for the kids to go to the park. Nard is fixated on playing with spoons. I always take the silver spoons from him and replace them with plastic spoons. They are on the second shelf in the cabinet."

"I still don't see why you feel like you need to get away for a weekend without us. You never needed any damn solitude before." Bernard protested.

"Please don't do this." Rhonda begged. "Please don't. I'm going to see Shemeka. I haven't seen her since she left. You know that's my gal. Besides, all we have done lately is argue about Nard. We need this weekend apart to help us get things in perspective."

"Perspective!" He yelled. "I have things in perspective but if this is what you want to do then by all means go ahead and do it."

Rhonda knew that Bernard didn't want her to leave but she refused to let him make her feel guilty. The only guilt she felt was about leaving the kids for the weekend but one weekend wouldn't hurt. It would be the first weekend she had ever left them but it wasn't like she was making it a habit.

"The kids are still asleep so I won't wake them. Since Dean's bus comes after you leave, she will have to be a car rider today. The bus driver and school have both been notified. They'll keep her in the office until you get there to pick her up after work. Kiss my babies for me and tell them Mama loves them."

Bernard grabbed Rhonda's suitcase. "I'll take this to the car for you. Damn! What did you pack? You act like you are going to be gone for a month."

Rhonda laughed. "You know how I am when it comes to packing. I'd never leave my babies for that long. This weekend is hard enough."

"It can't be that hard. You're leaving." He responded.

"Bernard, we've already been through this. I have to do this for me. I'll see you Sunday." She kissed Bernard on the forehead and walked to the door. "Take care of my babies." She left the door open as she walked to her car and drove away.

Chapter 20

The sun was bright, almost blinding as it crept through the windows and lit the room. *Damn!* Bernard thought. *The fuckin weatherman messed this shit up. Talking about seventy-five percent chance of showers. Yeah. Right! As they say, he is the only person who has a job where he can be wrong and still get paid.*

Bernard woke Dean up and gave her the clothes Rhonda had left out for her to wear. He was glad she had taken her bath before going to bed. Nard on the other hand had not been as compliant. He was used to Rhonda bathing him. When Bernard put him in the tub and tried to wash him, Nard would not release the washcloth. Bernard took another washcloth from the linen closet since Nard wanted to play with the first one. It was upsetting to Bernard. He wanted a miracle even though there was no miracle. He dealt with special needs kids on a daily basis, yet he was not able to cope with his own child's disability. He didn't want Nard to play with spoons, sticks and washcloths. He wanted his son to play with trucks, cars and army men.

After he had finally gotten Nard bathed and dried, Dean was a big help to him. Nard sat on the floor with two plastic spoons. His sister got on the floor with two plastic spoons and played with him. At first Bernard wanted to scream at her but he knew she was only trying to help. Besides, he thought to himself, *If Nard can't come into our world, maybe we should explore his world.*

The kids got up from the floor to eat the fruit loops Bernard had prepared for them. When they had finished eating, Bernard assisted his son in brushing his teeth. Dean brushed her teeth and was excited about going to the park.

"I wish Mama was here with us." She told her daddy.

"I know Baby, but she's gone to visit your aunt Meka. She'll be home tomorrow. I know you miss her. I miss her too, but we're going to have fun at the park like Mama wants us to do."

"Yippee Nard. We are going to the park. I'm going to push you in the swings too." Dean was ecstatic but Nard seemed to ignore his sister.

"Dean. Listen Honey." Bernard walked over to where she was. "I know that you love your brother and want to help him. It's going to be a little challenging but we can do this. What I want us to do is start working on eye contact. Whenever you talk to him, stand in front of him and look at him or take his hand and try to get his attention so he'll look at you. Can you do that for daddy?"

"Yeah! I can do that Daddy." She answered.

"Okay Honey. That's my big girl." He kissed Dean on the cheek. "Grab your brother and let's go."

When the car was loaded and he was driving to the park, Bernard wondered what his life would be like if he didn't have children. Rhonda had actually been a trooper to accept both of his children by Nikki. Especially since she didn't have any of her own. Maybe it was time to do something about that. Maybe when she returned from her trip they would discuss her getting pregnant. She was a good mom and patient with the kids. They both loved her and he couldn't ask for a better mom. In fact, he couldn't ask for a better wife.

"Damn!" He thought out loud.

"What's wrong Daddy?" Dean asked curiously.

"Oh! Nothing Honey. Daddy just thought about something." He had not meant to be verbal. His thoughts were for him only. He thought about how Nikki had disguised herself and coaxed him into being with her. She wasn't stupid. She knew exactly what she was doing. How the hell could he not finish after she had licked and lapped all over his magic stick? Her mouth had to be made different from any woman he had ever met. When she took his magic stick in her mouth, something went all through his body. It was like electricity. The bitch was crazy as hell but she was good. And just thinking about her mouth on his magic stick made it start to come to life.

This is crazy. Bernard thought as he grabbed his crotch. *Let me get my mind back to where it's supposed to be.*

When they got to the park and out of the car, the ducks immediately flocked to the newcomers in their territory. Nard seemed frightened and his daddy picked him up. Dean fed the ducks the popcorn she had bought for them.

Bernard walked over to the swings with Dean and Nard. "Dean, I'll be right over there on the bench if you need me. Y'all have fun."

She put her brother in the toddler swing and gave him a push. He didn't smile but the back and forth movement seemed soothing to him.

"Excuse me lil girl." A dark skinned woman with a burgundy wig approached Dean. She had on dark shades and wore a straw hat. "Who is this handsome young man you are pushing? Is this your brother?" She asked.

"Yes Ma'am."

"Well that doesn't seem fair to you Sweetie. Why don't you go ahead and get on the big swing? I will push your brother for a while."

"Oh! Okay. Thanks." Dean got on the big swing and left the woman pushing Nard. It had been years since she had seen Nikki and with the disguise, Dean didn't recognize Nikki as the woman who had given birth to her.

Nikki pushed Nard on the swing. How are you doing today?" She asked him. There was no response. "Do you hear me talking to you? I asked you how are you doing today?"

Nard relaxed on the swing, enjoying the motion and unaware that Nikki was getting agitated. She pushed the swing a little harder. "I'm going to ask you one more damn time lil boy. I don't like to be fuckin ignored!"

He didn't mind that the swing was going faster. His facial expression didn't change until Nikki stopped the swing completely. She walked to the front of the swing and with one hand squeezed both of Nard's cheeks hard. "Do you understand English, you lil bastard?"

Nikki suddenly felt excruciating pain in her upper thigh. "Leave my brother alone you mean woman. You take your hands off him!"

She grabbed her upper thigh where Dean had bitten her. "You fuckin brat!"

"Help! Help!" Dean screamed loudly. Parents and children looked in the direction that the screams were coming from. Bernard ran to his daughter's aid while Nikki ran towards the park entrance.

"A mean woman tried to hurt Nard. She put her hands on him." Dean pointed in Nikki's direction. "Look! There she is."

Bernard ran behind Nikki after asking another parent to keep an eye on the kids. His days of running track paid off. He was fast. He caught Nikki before she could reach Karen's car. He grabbed her arm and swung her around. "Nikki!"

He was shocked. "What the hell did you do to my kids? I'm calling the police on your ass if somebody hasn't already done it. Why the hell are you at the park? I told you to stay away from my family. Your ass is about to get locked back up again. You have done enough to destroy my life. You are not going to destroy these kids."

"I'm not. I promise. I was trying to talk to him and he kept ignoring me. You know how I hate to be ignored. Let me go before somebody mess around and call the police." She attempted to pull away from Bernard.

He tightened his grip on her. "No Nikki. I'm not letting you go."

Nikki looked Bernard straight in his eyes. "Muthafucka I am not asking you to let me go. I am fuckin telling you to let me go. Or do you want that wife of yours to know how you fucked me? And how you enjoyed it."

Bernard loosed his grip on Nikki. "Just stay the hell away from my family."

Nikki got in Karen's car and drove away. Bernard walked back to the kids feeling defeated. *When in the hell are they going to catch that bitch? I never should have fucked her. Damn! What the hell was I thinking? I wasn't thinking at all. If Rhonda finds out, she'll leave me. No she won't. She'll kill me. Hell. If Nikki's pregnant again, I'll kill my damn self. When Rhonda gets back tomorrow, we're definitely going to have to work on having that baby.*

"Daddy, did you catch that mean woman?" Dean was anxious to find out if her daddy had caught the woman who tried to hurt her brother. "Did you Daddy? Did you get her?"

"I'm afraid not Honey. She's long gone but I don't think she will bother your brother or you again."

Bernard thanked the woman for watching the kids. Nard didn't seem fazed by the incident. Bernard picked him up in one arm and took Dean by the hand. "Whadda ya say, we go to McDonalds and eat lunch? I bet that I can eat more fries than you."

Dean laughed. "I bet you can't. I'm the French Fry Queen."

Bernard smiled. He had gotten Dean's mind off the mean woman. Hopefully, neither of them ever had to see Nikki again. He prayed that she would just disappear.

Chapter 21

Anthony got out of his car and opened the door to the cabin.

"Hey der Sexy. I've missed ya. I'm glad ya was able ta make it. I wuz wondrin if ya wuz gon be able ta get away."

"If I couldn't make it, I would have called you. I needed this weekend."

"Well we bof needed it. Jessica ben actin kinda funny. I don know if she suspec sumthin or wat." Anthony said.

"Wait a minute. Before we start talking about other people Anthony, don't you think you should give me a proper welcome?"

"Well, since dis is ya cabin, it seems like ya da one dat shud be givin me da welcome, but brin ya sexy ass ova here and give me a kiss." Anthony licked his lips with his tongue. All the way to the cabin he had thought about how great it was going to be to get away for the weekend and get some great loving. He got a rush out of living on the edge and taking chances.

I wonda wat Jessica is thinkin. Do she really thin sumthin is goin on? Wud she call off da weddin if she foun out. It really wudn't matter cuz I don love hur. I just feel obligated ta hur.

Anthony was enjoying the kiss. It was soft and passionate. Then a tear. "Oh damn!" He spoke softly. "Ya done tore anutha shirt off of me."

"It's fine. I'll buy you another one. Right now I want you to get out of the rest of your clothes. I want to kiss you all over before I suck your dick."

Anthony moaned as he enjoyed having his neck sucked on and the kisses on his chest. He unzipped his pants and let them fall to the floor. After he stepped out of his underwear, he stood in the middle of the floor naked. "Put my dick in your mouth." He begged.

His manhood was hard. "Oh damn! Ya know how ta handle a dick. I swear ya do. Umm…shit! Dat feels gud. Suck dat dick."

Anthony really enjoyed getting his dick sucked. He felt powerful to be fucking someone in the mouth while they were on their knees where they could look up to him. Prison tried to strip him of his manhood but he was a man. He was in control. He took care of his.

"Suck it harder." He demanded. "Put all of this dick in your mouth."

Anthony felt good but he would never cum without making sure his partner was satisfied. That shit wouldn't be right. Not to just leave somebody hanging.

"Okay Sexy. Get on da bed. I'm ready ta put dis dick up in ya. Do ya want ya favorite position? Get on dose hands and knees and let me give ya wat ya came fer." He let out a sigh of pleasure as his dick went in. While his dick went in and out Anthony craved the power of submissiveness.

"Is dis dick gud ta ya? He asked.

"Yeah! It's good."

"Has any otha man eva fucked ya like dis?"

"No! Oh shit Anthony. Oh, your dick makes me fee…el goo…od. Oh yeah!"

"Do I satisfy ya? Augh …ah!"

"Yes! You satisfy me. Your dick is sat…is…fy…ing."

"Tell me." Anthony said loudly. "Tell me now!

"What?"

"Dat ya don wan no otha di...ick but mine.!" He responded.

"Yours Anthony. Ju...st you...rs. Oh day...am! I'm cum...ming."

"Ou! Ouu! Me tooooo. I'm with ya Se...x...cy." Anthony held on until he was drained.

"Ah! Dat felt gud. I love ya. Do ya know dat?" He moved over on the bed and put a pillow under his head. "Lay rite here in my arms. Ya dint anszer me. Do ya know dat I love ya?

"Yes, Anthony. I believe that you love me but come on now. You and I both know that we can never be together. We shouldn't be together now. I don't know how we even got to this point. Do you know there was a time when I didn't even like you?"

"Why? Why dint ya like me? Ya dint even know me?"

"Well yeah. You are right but we do have a tendency to prejudge people. I'm guilty of that. But no where in my wildest of dreams did I think we would end up in a relationship."

Anthony rolled over on his side. "Wow! And nobody wudn't dream ya wud hav da connects ya hav. We don made a lota money. I needed dat boost but ya don even need da money. Ya already hav it made."

"For right now, but you never know what the future may bring."

"Ima always gon take care of ya like I said. We in dis tagatha but if anythin eva go down, I gotcha. Ya got too much ta lose. Let's take a nap. Wheneva we wake up I might wanna hit it in da shower."

Anthony rolled over on the bed while his mind drifted to Brandi. *Damn! Dis wud kill Brandi. She's cool tho and I don wanna hurt hur but she hurt me first. I still can't believ she turned hur back on a brotha like dat. Hell. I needed hur. I really did. It wuz a struggle ta keep from goin crazy in dat hell hole. Den she had da nerve ta bail on a nigga. Nah! I'm sorry. I'll fuck hur weneva I decide. Not wen she decide. She don run nunthin here. I'm rite here wit who I love.*

He looked to his left. *I love ya and sum how I'm gon hav ya.*

Chapter 22

Karen was half asleep when she heard the keys turn in the door. Nikki never tried to be quiet when she entered the house. She slammed the keys on the counter and flopped down in one of the kitchen chairs. She was obviously upset.

"Is that you Nikki?" Karen asked from her bedroom. She prayed every night that Jesus would remove Nikki from her house. *Any way you choose to remove her Lord.* Karen would pray. *I know that I was wrong for getting involved with her. I should never have let a patient manipulate me. Please get me out of this and I will never cross the line again. I'll be in church every time the doors open and I will even be on time.*

Now that she prayed every night, all she had to do was wait. She couldn't rush God. She knew that He would move in his own time but she sure did want Him to hurry up.

"Who the hell else would it be? Don't be stupid." Nikki yelled back into the room. "I'm fuckin pissed and I'm stressed. Get Lance on the phone and tell him to get his ass over here. RIGHT DAMN NOW!!"

Karen got out of bed wondering what had set Nikki off this time. It didn't take much to light her fuse. Life was miserable for everybody when Nikki was upset and Karen hated it when Nikki was stressed.

Those were the times when she most often became abusive and thought sex was a stress reliever.

She dialed Lance's phone number and got his voice mail. "Hello Lance. This is Karen. Nikki needs to see you as soon as possible. She's in one of her moods. I don't know what happened but I suggest you get here on the double." She hung up the telephone.

"Did you get him"" Nikki asked as she slowly walked down the hall.

"No" Karen answered. "I didn't get an answer but I left him a message."

"Damn him. I have told his ass about not answering his phone. He better get his ass over here if he knows what's good for him." She walked to Karen's room and strolled over to where Karen was standing at the foot of the bed. She pushed her backwards.

"Lay your ass here and let me taste my fruit."

Karen slid back on the bed. She hated Nikki but at the same time, Nikki made her feel good. She couldn't understand that. How could she get such enjoyment from someone she despised? Karen spread her legs and positioned herself so Nikki could eat her fruit. Nikki didn't waste any time and Karen relaxed while Nikki made her feel good.

"Um…" Karen moaned softly as she grabbed Nikki's head. "Oh yes Mama. Ah! Mama!" Karen pulled Nikki's hair. It felt so good that she couldn't help it. But Nikki stopped eating the fruit.

"So you want to fuckin pull hair huh? Is that what you want to do?"

"No Mama. I'm sorry. I didn't mean to hurt you. Did I hurt you? I'm really sorry."

"I know damn well that your ass is sorry." Nikki closed Karen's legs. "You sorry ass bitch."

"Ouch! Oh my goodness Nikki! Please stop. What the hell is wrong with you." She exclaimed as Nikki grabbed the hairs from her fruit and pulled them.

Nikki continued to gather bunches of hair and yank. She didn't care that she was hurting Karen.

"Stop Nikki. Please stop!"

"Ain't no damn stopping Bitch. You want to pull hair don't you? Well this damn fruit is going to be bald when I finish with it." Nikki's voice was deep and frightening. "You motherfuckin-" The doorbell interrupted Nikki's threats.

"Sweetheart, someone is at the door. It's probably Lance." Nikki suddenly changed.

Karen looked out the peephole and saw a girl standing on the porch holding Girl Scout cookies. She didn't usually buy the cookies but welcomed the chance to get away from Nikki.

When she returned to the bedroom, Nikki was standing in the middle of the floor. "Come here." She told Karen.

Karen was scared to move, not quite knowing what to expect from the psycho. It wouldn't be out of the ordinary for Nikki to knock the hell out of her as soon as she was within reach. Karen took her time walking, what seemed like the long mile. She flinched when Nikki stretched her arms forth. She embraced Karen and squeezed her tightly.

"I'm so sorry Baby." Nikki kissed her face and neck. "I just don't understand why you like to upset me. You know that's not right. Sometimes I think you are trying to spoil it. I can't let you do that my dear. Do you understand?"

"I understand Mama. I'm not trying to spoil it." Karen looked towards the window. "I think I heard a car door."

Nikki peeped out to see Lance walking up the sidewalk. She quickly went to open the door. "What the fuck took you so damn long? Didn't you get my message that I needed to see your damn ass?" Nikki pointed her finger in his face.

What a damn coward. Karen thought. *He's a real bitch. There's no way that he can be that damn much in love. I thought that black men prided themselves on being strong. He's a poor excuse for a black man. He would fit better under the category of vertebrae.*

"Yes Nikki. I was at the shop getting my oil changed. I came as soon as I got your message. What's up?"

"What's up? Every damn thing is up. I need to see my friend Rhonda. I haven't been able to see her since my escape. I'm about to go crazy with all this damn sneaking around!" Nikki yelled at him.

"What do you want me to do? What do you need?" Lance seemed concerned.

Nikki started to cry. Karen and Lance both gazed at the pitiful woman who stood before them.

"I need to be with my lover and my kids. It's not fair. Rhonda is with that muthafucka and she should be with me. I should be raising those damn kids." She tried to compose herself. "You have to get the kids for me Lance. You have to bring them here."

Lance took two steps backward. "Nikki, I know that you aren't asking me to kidnap your kids are you? There is no way you can be asking me to do that."

"And where the hell is he going to take the kidnapped kids?" Karen questioned. "Mama, I know that you love your kids but if Lance kidnaps them, the place will be swarming with cops. And my neighbors know that I don't have kids. In fact, the most activity I ever had here was the chaos I've been dealing with since you came and Lance has been popping up like popcorn. Children would be a dead give away and then people will find out that you've been hiding here."

"You're right Karen. Maybe we need to find another place. And Rhonda. You will have to kidnap her also. That way we can make it look like she left that sorry ass limp dick husband of hers. How soon can you get us a place Lance?"

Thank you Jesus. You came through. I will be there Sunday and on time. Karen thought.

Lance fell on his knees. "No Nikki. Don't make me do this. Please don't. There has to be another way. I've done everything you have asked me to do because I love you." He stopped himself. He didn't mean to tell Nikki how much he loved her. He was trying to get his feelings under control or at least understand them. Was it real love or was it the way Nikki made him feel? *Damn!* He thought. *What in the hell made me say that?*

"Love?" Nikki laughed. "Love? What the hell does love have to do with any of this? It's all about need and right now, I need for you to take care of a few things for me. That's what I need. Now what do you need? Do you need for Mama to take care of you?"

Lance didn't answer.

"Bring your ass on in the bedroom so we can discuss it."

Karen watched as Nikki followed Lance to the bedroom. "Come on Karen" Nikki said firmly. "Bring your ass on back here with us."

"I wish I could." Karen answered quickly. "But I have to shower and get ready for work."

Lance had a smug smile on his face as he spoke. "I thought this was your day off Karen."

Smart ass son of a bitch. "It's suppose to be but Ms. Covington called in. She can't make it today. They asked me to cover and I said I would. I can use the extra money."

Nikki held on to Lance as they headed for the bedroom. His smile never vanished. He was excited to know he would be getting a piece of Nikki.

Karen looked at him in amazement. *Has this dumb ass pussy whipped man forgotten that Nikki just asked him to be involved in a kidnapping? Damn! How stupid can a man be?*

"See you when you get off from work." Nikki glanced back over her shoulder at Karen who stood there with a look of confusion on her face. She went on into the bedroom with Lance. His excitement was evident by the bulge in his pants. She unzipped his pants and after pulling out his rod and massaging it, she fell to her knees.

"Whew! Lance, this thing is huge. Baby, you don't know how I have missed this." She licked around the head while securing the base firmly in her hand. "We have something special between us. I didn't mean to act like I did in the living room but I don't want to make Karen jealous. I think she has a crush on me, and I do want to respect her since I am living in her house. I love you Lance."

She took him in her mouth and then out. Lance felt as if he could soar. He had wanted to hear her say those words. He always felt that Nikki loved him but just wouldn't admit it. He thought it but he needed to know it. Now, he could feel confident in leaving his wife. "Oh Nikki." He moaned. "I love you too. Damn. You are sucking the hell out of my dick. Oh…shiiit!"

Lance felt good. They could call Nikki crazy all they wanted to. Crazy or not, she was an expert. She knew how to satisfy a man. He didn't want to cum yet. He wanted to be inside her. How could he keep a fine woman like Nikki if he didn't make sure she was satisfied?

"Ah! Ho…o…old up! I'm not…ready…to cum…yet."

Nikki stopped sucking Lance just as he was ready to spill a load. She stood in front of him and slowly came out of her clothes. He admired the beautiful, full figured, dark skinned woman who stood before him. She climbed into bed and stretched out both arms in front of her.

"Come here Lance. I want you to kiss me."

Lance got in bed next to Nikki and felt like he had died and woke up in Heaven. She kissed him with those scrumptious lips. "Words can't describe the way I feel about you Baby. Do you really love me? I mean like, you are serious aren't you?"

"Yes Nikki. I'm serious. I really love you." He spoke softly.

"Well if you really love me handsome man, you would help me get to see my kids. I don't believe you love me if you don't help me. Please. If you truly love me, then prove it. You don't really have to kidnap the kids. Start by bringing them to me and we will go from there."

"I will." He replied. "I love you so much Nikki and I will prove it to you."

Just like a damn man. Suck the muthafuckas dick, tell him you love him, and you can lead him to West Hell and back. It won't be long now Rhonda. "Thanks Lance. I love you and I knew I could count on you."

Chapter 23

Rhonda was deeply engaged in thought when the ringing telephone startled her. She looked at the caller ID. Brandi was calling from her cell phone.

"Hello...Oh! I didn't know you were off today. Sure we can do lunch. What time? Works for me. I'll be there." She hung up the telephone. *Um...wonder what that's about? Last time we talked she got all beside herself because of my remark about Anthony. I hope this is not a repeat performance. The nerve of her, saying Anthony wouldn't fuck me.*

Rhonda thought about Brandi. The two had been friends since school. They had gone through a lot together. She remembered when Brandi first got involved with Anthony. She couldn't stand him and she and Shemeka had tried to talk Brandi out of dating him because of his reputation. Anthony was not only a drug dealer but he was a lady's man and everybody knew it.

Brandi hadn't listened to her friends. She seemed to see something in Anthony that was invisible to those around her. In spite of what her family or anyone said, Brandi was determined to be in a relationship with Anthony.

Rhonda was thinking about her friend when the buzzer rang. "Yes?" she spoke into the intercom.

"Mrs. Simpson, it's Marcus. I have a certified letter for you which requires your signature."

"Sure Marcus. I'll buzz you in." Rhonda met Marcus at the door. He had been her mail carrier for the last seven months. She didn't like him at first because she thought he was arrogant and conceited. After getting to know him, she realized he was nothing like she thought. He had impressed her one day before Nard started daycare. He had taken a special interest in Nard and she saw how patient and kind he was.

"Okay Mrs. Simpson." Marcus placed an "X" on the paper and handed her the clipboard. "Sign here please."

Rhonda signed for the letter. "Wait a minute." She told Marcus. She picked up her purse and gave him a twenty-dollar bill before closing the door. When Rhonda looked at the envelope, she recognized Nikki's handwriting. It was a bit unnerving to be receiving, yet another letter from Nikki. She tore the envelope open and read.

Dear Rhonda,

I miss you. It won't be long now and I will be eating the hell out of that cookie. Please be patient. I miss you. Thanks for not letting the cookie crumble. I know that you have kept it for Mama. I can tell because the way Bernard fucked me in the hotel a few weeks ago, I knew he hadn't been getting much at home. (I have enclosed the hotel receipt so you can inquire about it.)

I didn't want his ass. That shit wasn't good to me. You are the one I want. And you are the one I am going to have. We are going to be a family. Mama will take care of everything.

In the meantime, my love, I need for you to cum with me when I cum. At 8:00 each night I need for you to put your finger in that cookie. Play with that cookie, work that finger, and rub that clit until you cream. Think about me while you are doing that. After you get the cream on your finger I want you to stick your finger in your mouth just like licking the cream from an Oreo. Think about how sweet that cookie is and how Mama is going to feast on it real soon. At 8:00 I will be doing the same thing. That's how we must do until we are able to get together. Keep it tight for me Baby.

Love ya much,

Nikki Boo

Rhonda looked at the envelope and pulled out the receipt, which she had apparently missed before. She wasn't worried about Nikki and all the crazy stuff Nikki said she was going to do to her. Rhonda was sure there was no way that Nikki could get to her. What concerned her was the hotel receipt and how Bernard could have fucked Nikki behind her back.

She looked at the receipt she held in her trembling hands. Nikki wasn't lying. She had no reason to make anything up on Bernard. *That lying, cheating ass son-of-a-bitch. How dare he? How did he get up with Nikki? Did he have anything to do with her escape? How the hell did he pull it off?*

Rhonda didn't know what the hell to think. She didn't know what to do. Should she confront Bernard or should she just sat back and try to catch him. And why would she want to do anything. He wasn't satisfying her. He was like most other men. It was okay for them to fuck around but if they found out that somebody was getting some of their stuff, the bastards couldn't take it. She decided not to say anything.

When Rhonda got to the restaurant, Brandi had just parked and was getting out of her car. She looked cute in her jean outfit and her fat ass got her a lot of attention. The man in the parking lot looked at her like she was filet mignon. The extra attention always flattered her even though she was not one of those girls who would easily give it up.

"Hey girl." She said as Rhonda walked over and greeted her with a hug. The two women walked in together. After being seated, they both ordered lemonade to drink.

"Rhonda, before we get our food, I want to apologize about the last time. I'm really sorry. It's a wonder you didn't blank on me. I know that you look out for my best interest and wouldn't tell me anything wrong. I love Anthony but you my girl. No man is ever going to come between us. Remember our vow?"

"Yeah, I remember that." Rhonda answered. "The three of us made that vow a long time ago. We're straight. Anthony is like the typical man. That's why I said if I were like that, he would fuck me in a heartbeat. That's just how men are but that still didn't give me the right to talk to you the way I did. I guess I was just surprised to find out you were seeing him again."

"Rhonda, he is not a bad person. He just made a mistake. Everybody makes mistakes."

"Tell me about it." Rhonda responded in a soft voice. "I've certainly made my share. It's too bad we can't go back and change some of the things we have done. But we can't. Once it is done, it becomes history."

"Sounds like to me that you have something on your mind. What's up? You want to talk about it?"

"Nah Brandi." Rhonda avoided eye contact with her friend as she looked around the restaurant. "Where the hell did our waitress go? I'm ready to order."

"Here she comes." Brandi answered.

The bright and bubbly waitress smiled as she approached their booth. After taking their order she scurried to the back.

Rhonda sought to change the subject from Anthony. "We're going to have to get together and visit Meka to make sure she is on the right track.

Brandi nodded in agreement. "I really miss her."

Rhonda took a swallow of her lemonade. When she looked up, she nearly got strangled and spit the lemonade out of her mouth and across the table barely missing Brandi.

"Are you alright?" Brandi asked her. "You look like you've seen a ghost."

"No. I'm fine." She lied as she tried to regain her composure. "It just went down the wrong way."

She looked up again and Nikki blew her a kiss before walking out the door.

Chapter 24

Brandi felt good. She and Rhonda had cleared the air and there were no hard feelings between them. Rhonda may never like Anthony but at least she respected him as being Brandi's man. Brandi couldn't help but to wonder what was going on with Rhonda. One minute she was herself and the next minute, she seemed to get lost in herself.

If she needs to talk, she will when she gets ready. Right now, life is good and I am just going to enjoy Anthony. It's more relaxing to be at Anthony's place since I don't have to worry about Jessica dropping in. He never said why they called the wedding off. Brandi watched Anthony while he slept.

I love you so much, I wonder if Jessica found out you were seeing me and ended things. Or maybe you were the one who called things off. It's good to be here with you but I hate like hell that I couldn't make you cum. I wanted to make you feel as good as you made me feel but you didn't really seem interested. I guess you were tired.

Brandi pulled the covers up over her and snuggled under Anthony. She was where she wanted to be. She loved Anthony more than life. She was about to doze off when she heard the vibrating of a cell phone. Anthony's phone slightly moved as it vibrated on the nightstand. *Who the hell would be calling him at 2:47 a.m. unless there is an emergency? It might be important. Maybe I should answer it. Nah! He'd have a damn fit. He doesn't play that. The last thing in the world I want to do is argue over a cell phone.*

Brandi eased the covers off her and slowly got out of bed, being careful not to wake Anthony. Curiosity got the best of her and she wanted to know who was calling. She tipped to the other side of the bed and examined the phone. One missed call. *Caller Private.*

She walked back to the bed and quietly slid under the covers. Her mind was full of questions. She didn't want to upset Anthony but she didn't understand who would be calling him that time of morning? Brandi tossed and turned until she finally fell asleep.

At 6:20 a.m. Brandi was awakened when Anthony sat up in bed. She heard the sound of people running in the house.

Someone shouted, "Police! Get down!"

"It's the police!" Anthony told her. "Get on the floor!" They both got on the floor. Anthony took the nine-millimeter machine type pistol, which was on the floor and threw it towards the closet.

"Police! Search warrants!" Someone shouted as two of the officers opened the door of the master bedroom with guns drawn.

"Where's the search warrant?" Anthony asked.

The officer ignored him. "Is there anyone else in the house?"

"No." He answered.

Anthony could hear the other officers going through the house. Brandi remained speechless as she lay on the floor wearing only a short nightee. One of the officers picked up the loaded nine millimeter that was in front of the closet.

"Get up!" An officer shouted. After stripping the covers off the bed, Brandi was allowed to sit on the bed while the officers observed Anthony getting dressed. Ten minutes later a female officer arrived and Brandi was allowed to get dressed.

The two were taken into the kitchen to sat while the house was being searched. An officer retrieved $2,740.00 from the nightstand beside Anthony's bed. He placed it in a small plastic bag. Another officer handed Anthony a copy of the warrant. He and Brandi looked at it together.

"Anthony." She whispered. "What the hell is going on here?"

Before he could answer her, one of the officers retrieved a small plastic bag, which contained white, rocky looking stuff. He handed it to another officer.

"Oh my goodness Anthony. What is that?" Brandi panicked.

"Calm down." He whispered. "Datz not mine. Redd musta lef it here."

"I told you he was bad news. I tried to tell you not to deal with him." Tears started to roll down her face.

Officers walked back and forth through the house carrying items. A 12-gauge shotgun, a SKS rifle, a Ruger mini 14 and a AP-9. Brandi's heart beat faster each time an officer walked by her. She didn't understand why Anthony wasn't sweating. *Where the hell did all those guns come from? What the hell has Anthony gotten me into? I have to be at the V.A. Medical Center by 8:00.* "May I please use the telephone?" She asked as two officers walked by. "I need to call my job."

"Sorry Ma'am but you just need to sat there."

She looked at Anthony. "Tell me the truth. Am I going to be charged? Am I going to jail? I'll have to call Rhonda to get me out."

"No!" Anthony answered quickly. "Ya ain't dun nunthin. Stop dat whining. I gotcha!"

From where they sat in the kitchen, neither Brandi nor Anthony could see the officers in the master bedroom. One officer came out with a large bag which contained smaller bags of the white stuff.

"Oh shit!" Anthony mumbled as the officers asked them to stand. After he was instructed to place his hands behind his back, Anthony was handcuffed and read his Miranda rights. Brandi was not arrested and watched in silence as Anthony was put in the patrol car and it cruised away from the house.

Chapter 25

Karen was delighted to have the house all to herself. Although she couldn't afford it, she sprung for Nikki a hotel room for the weekend. Nikki had declared she had some personal business to take care of. *Maybe someone will recognize her in the lobby. They'll call the police and then I will be rid of her.*

As if Nikki was reading her mind, she said, "You'll have to get the room in your name Karen. Nothing fancy. No lobbies. I need a hotel with outside room entrance. Oh! And I will need your car also. Mama has some things to take care of."

Nikki backed her up against the wall and gave her a wet tongue kiss before leaving. Then with a smug smile on her face, she pinched Karen on the ass. "Umph! Hold this fruit for Mama and don't let it spoil."

It had been raining all day. Karen curled up in bed and polished her toes as she enjoyed the soothing sound of the rain going pitter-patter on the tin roof of her house. *I hope Nikki never comes back. I swear that I can't take too much more of her. Why did I even let them talk me into this? No. I'm wrong. They didn't talk me into this. They blackmailed me. I was stupid. I could have lost my job for being with Nikki even though it would have been her word against mine. Now I stand the risk of losing my freedom. On top of that, the fool has a gun.*

The ringing doorbell startled Karen. She had not expected company. "Yes?" She asked as she walked to the door.

"It's Lance."

What the hell does he want? Karen asked herself before opening the door.

Lance stood there soaked from head to toe and holding two bags. Karen held the door with one hand while stepping aside so Lance could enter. "What are you doing here Lance?" She asked, trying to sound casual.

"I thought I'd bring you and Nikki a bite to eat. I hope you gals are hungry. I have ribs, slaw, potato salad, baked beans and even a loaf of garlic bread. Where's Nikki?"

"Oh! You mean she didn't tell you? Didn't you notice that my car isn't out there? Nikki's gone for the weekend. I put her up at the Budget Inn. She's in room #17 if you need her." The expression on Lance's face reflected his disappointment. It was as if he was a helium balloon and she had stuck a pin in him.

"No Karen." I didn't know she was leaving for the weekend." Lance answered quickly while he stood in the center of the kitchen floor dripping water all over the tile. "I thought she wanted to lay low. If she messes around and get caught, I will be ruined. That will be the end of me."

"Lance, calm down. Why don't you go to the bathroom and get out of those wet clothes? I'll throw them in the dryer for you and we'll eat some of this food. No need in it going to waste."

"Yeah, I see that I have created a small puddle here on your floor." Lance said after he placed the food on the table.

"You know where the bathroom is. Just hand me your clothes out the door." Karen walked down the hall behind Lance. "There are some towels in the linen closet. You can use one to wrap up in until your clothes are dry."

Within minutes, Lance was handing his wet clothes out the door. Karen put them in the dryer and was taking food out the bags when Lance walked into the kitchen with a towel wrapped around his waste. "Need some help?"

"No. I'm good." Karen responded. "Just getting this food out so we can eat the ribs while they are still warm."

Lance gazed out the kitchen window. "I see that it hasn't slacked up yet. That rain is really coming down."

"Yeah. I know but it sounds good beating on the roof. It's relaxing. I can't explain it but the rain soothes me and puts me in a certain mood."

Lance shifted his attention from the rain to Karen. He had never really noticed her before but she was a beautiful Latino woman. She had on a pair of shorts and a tube top with no bra. Her nipples made an indention in the tube top. *Um…wonder what it would feel like to have one of those damn tits in my mouth.* He let his hand brush slightly across his manhood.

"Let's have a seat and enjoy some of this great looking food you brought." Karen felt sorry for him. He had wanted to surprise Nikki and she hadn't even had the decency to let him know she wasn't going to be there.

Lance held out a chair for Karen before he took a seat. She looked sexy as hell to him. Why hadn't he noticed her before? Usually her hair was pinned up but today her hair was down and hanging on her shoulders. All he could think about was what it would be like to stick his dick in her. Just one time. Just to feel the lips of her pussy around his dick. *Damn! Get yourself together.* Lance told himself as he could feel the stiffness in his manhood.

"These ribs are delicious!" Karen told Lance while she licked her sticky fingers one at a time.

He didn't answer. He was in his own zone watching her. *The way she is licking those fingers. In and out of her mouth like that. Licking all in between her fingers. I wish I could stick my hard dick in her mouth right now,* He thought.

"Lance! Lance! Earth to Lance." She teased. "You've barely touched your food. Aren't you hungry?"

"No. Not really. I just wanted to do something nice for yall." He answered.

"Oh wow! Well that was sweet of you. You're not so bad after all Lance. I sure did enjoy mine. I'm going to straighten up the kitchen. Your clothes are going to be dry in a little bit." Karen stood and started clearing the table."

"I'll help you." Lance stood and the towel that had been wrapped around him fell to the floor. His manhood was rock hard and impossible for Karen not to notice. She gazed at his erection and tried to do it unnoticed. She hadn't been with a man in a minute and seeing that stiff rod made her moist. She wanted to turn away and not look at it but she was frozen in her tracks and unable to move.

Lance made no attempt to pick up the towel. Instead, he rushed to Karen and started kissing her. She responded by kissing back. If felt great. He stuck his hands in her shorts and fingered her while he kissed her,

"Um...um...!" She moaned in delight.

"Karen, can I have some?" Lance asked. "Please! Can I just have a little bit.?

"Lance, I don't know. That feels so good. Umph! Just finger fuck me. Let me come on your finger."

He stopped and took his hands out of her shorts. "Don't you want me to get mine too?"

"I do Lance but we shouldn't be doing this in the first place. I don't know what the hell got into me."

"So now you are going to stop huh? Just like that. are you really going to leave me like this?" He put his hands on his manhood, which had gotten so hard the veins were visible in it. "Let's at least go to the bedroom and talk about it. I feel kind of funny standing in your kitchen naked."

"Alright Lance. We'll talk." Karen agreed, but she knew what was going to happen.

Lance walked into her bedroom naked. When she entered the room, he kissed her again. "Let me have you Karen. I want you so bad. No strings attached. Please!" He begged.

Karen didn't resist when Lance slid her shorts down. She had been stressed out and needed to relieve the tension. She stepped her feet out of the shorts and turned back the covers on the bed. After getting in the center of the bed, she held her hands out to invite Lance. He put his arms under her legs and slid her to the very edge of the bed before falling on his knees to taste her.

Wow! He feels good but nothing like Nikki. She lay there and let him eat her fruit until he brought her to a climax. She kept her position at the edge of the bed while he stood. Lance put her legs over his shoulders and dove deep into her wet pool.

"Ah!" He said loudly as he felt the heat from her hot pussy surround his manhood. "This pussy feels good. Damn good." He was loud. "Oh Baby!" Lance screamed. "Umph! Talk to me Baby. Ah!" He continued to stroke. "Tell me this can be my pussy. Oh shiiit you feel good to me."

"YOU FUCKING SON-OF-A-BITCH! IT WAS MY DAMN FRUIT UNTIL YOU SPOILED IT!" Nikki screamed.

Neither of them had expected Nikki to come back but they both knew there would definitely be hell to pay.

Chapter 26

Brandi was distraught as she pulled in behind Rhonda's car. Rhonda was truly a good friend. She hadn't asked too many questions when Brandi called, asking her to come to the police station with bail money. Although she was a housewife and didn't work, Rhonda was rolling in money from her husband's inheritance. She had platinum credit cards and access to all of his finances.

I should have come to her right after all of this mess started. Brandi thought. At first, she felt like she could keep it quiet and let things die down. Now she was going to have to take a leave of absence from her job.

When the detectives and drug enforcement officers raided Anthony's house, she was nervous even though she had tried to remain calm. When they arrested Anthony for maintaining a dwelling for the sell and distribution of a controlled substance, she was blown away. But even though she had not been charged at the time, the stupid ass District Attorney's office later decided to charge her.

She got out of her car and followed Rhonda into the house. "Thank you for coming to get me Rhonda. I know that I owe you an explanation."

"You don't owe me anything." Rhonda answered. "If you want to talk. Fine. If you don't want to talk, fine. Would you like something to drink?"

"Yes! Please! I'm stressed out like hell. The usual." Rhonda fixed a drink for Brandi and one for herself. She sat down across from her friend.

"Last week, I was at Anthony's when the police raided his place. We were in bed one minute and the cops were running down the hall the next minute. I didn't know what was going on. They found drugs and guns in the house. They detained me while they searched the house for drugs. They let me go but for some reason, they turned around and decided to charge me later." She cried.

"Did you know he had all that stuff in the house?" Rhonda asked.

"No I didn't. Well I knew he had the gun but he told me that was for protection. And don't say it Rhonda. I know you are going to blame Anthony because you don't like him but please don't. Not today. I am not in the mood for it."

"Brandi, I was not going to blame him. You're a grown woman. Whatever he's doing, I'm sure he didn't mean to drag you into it. Hopefully things will work out for him and he'll get another chance."

"I just hope that all of this doesn't get to the hospital administrator." Brandi cried. "You know how fast things can spread."

"Yeah!" Rhonda said reassuringly. "But you didn't do anything so you should be fine. Have you seen Anthony since his arrest?"

"No. I'm not sure if he's out yet. I don't think so because he would have called." Brandi looked worried. She wondered if Anthony was ok. She knew that if she continued to talk about it she would get emotional.

"So how are things with you and Bernard?" She changed the subject. "Any better?"

"Hell no." Rhonda didn't hesitate to answer. "We disagree all the time over the kids. Dean is so bright she can always tell when there is friction even though we try to hide it from her. Nard does his own thing. He can't tell people's emotions but I know he can tell we love him. I just want him to learn at his own pace. And I think Bernard is trying to push him too hard."

"Well I am not trying to take sides Rhonda. You know I love you like a sister. But your husband is an exceptional children's teacher. He is certified and cross category. You know there are not a lot of teachers out there with his credentials. Maybe, he knows what he is talking about. He's not going to do anything that wouldn't be beneficial to his son."

"Maybe Brandi. I don't know but that's not all of it. He doesn't turn me on any more."

"Come on now Rhonda. Didn't you go through that same phase years ago where you said Bernard didn't turn you on? Don't you remember that you considered getting a separation from him? Is that where you're at again?"

"To be honest with you, I don't know where I'm at. Bernard and I had sex the other night. That's the way I refer to it now, because it is not making love. I was on my hands and knees. He knows that doggie style is my favorite position but he tells me that he wants me to get on top. I get on top and his ass is squirting in less than five minutes. Then, when I take a bath and leave, he wants to flip." Rhonda answered.

"Leave? What the hell?" Brandi responded. "Don't tell me that you are seeing somebody else."

"Girl please. Who the hell would I be seeing?"

"Rhonda, girl, I ain't mad at you one damn bit. It's a poor damn car that doesn't have a spare. Hell…if Bernard is not doing it for you then you have to do what it takes to get yours. I feel you."

"Stop Brandi. You are letting your imagination run wild. I had gone out to get some air and clear my head."

"If you say so." Brandi knew she might as well change the subject. If Rhonda had something going on, she wouldn't talk about it until she was ready. "When is the last time you talked to Meka? It's been a while since I heard from her. We are going to have to plan a trip to visit and check on her. You know that Meka is just a softie and it would be easy for someone to take advantage of her."

"I know but she has matured a lot. I think that Robert's death kind of did something to her. We do need to plan a visit though." Rhonda agreed.

The house phone rang while they were talking. Rhonda answered it. "Hello. I'm well. Thank you. How are you? Sure. That'll work. See you in an hour." She hung up the phone and turned to Brandi. "I don't mean to rush you but I'm trying to get some extra services for Nard and the woman just called with a cancellation so I'm going to take it."

"Oh, go ahead." Brandi stood. "I understand. I'll talk to you later."

The two embraced and Brandi left. As she drove away she thought. *Wonder if that is really where you are going Rhonda. I could be wrong but I wonder if you have a secret lover.*

Chapter 27

Anthony paced back and forth across the room. He couldn't believe the police had bust in on him like that. How could they possibly know what was going on with him unless somebody had snitched?

Hurry up and get ya sexy ass here, I sho do need ya. Anthony thought as he paced the floor.

It wasn't long until his doorbell rang. He answered it quickly.

"Anthony. Are you alright Boo?"

"I'm fine. Thanks fer goin my bail. I already no dat nobody can't find out ya got me out." He answered.

"What happened?"

"Me and Brandi wuz here in da bed and-"

"Yeah, but why was she here? You don't love her. You said you were going to ease away from her to keep from hurting her. I don't want to see Brandi hurt. You know that."

"I know dat. I don wan ta see her hurt either. She wuzn't pose ta be here. I'm not tryna drag her into dis. Ima take care of her lawyer and everythin." Anthony was remorseful.

"I'll take care of all of that for you. I have obtained you a lawyer out of Atlanta. He's the best. Just keep your mouth shut. Don't say anything without him present. They will try to get you to talk but exercise your 5th Amendment right."

"I know Sexy. I know how dat shit go. Gimme a kiss. I don wan ta thin bout dat mess. Ya know dat I wudn't use ya name in none of dis mess. I love ya. Ya know dat don ya?"

"Yes Anthony, I know you love me and would never put me out there like that. I have too much to lose. Nobody knows about us and we have to keep it that way."

Anthony walked towards the bedroom. "Come on. We can finish talking in here. Ima let ya back it up ta me." He smiled. "Dis is all I was thinkin bout wen dey had my ass on locks. It still confuse me dat we are tagather. I don no how dis happen but I love ya. I neva thot I'd love ya like dis." Anthony pulled back the covers on his bed. His rod had stiffened. He licked his lips and started to undress.

"You're right Anthony. It really is something how we got together considering the fact that I couldn't stand your ass. I didn't think you were right for Brandi. I thought you were going to bring her down. Now, look at me. Here I am with you. But I didn't plan for it to be this way."

"I no dis wuz not planned. I wuz actchilly surprise wen ya called and said ya had a bizness deal fer me. Wen ya said we cud both make money, I dint know wat ya wuz talkin bout. Ya already hav money available ta ya. No one wud eva thin." Anthony walked to the side of the bed. "Ben ova here on da bed and lemme give ya wat ya came here fer."

Anthony felt so proud to be in control. "Umph! Ya don no how much I missed dis. Do dis dick feel gud ta ya? Tell me ya love dis dick." Anthony demanded. "Tell me dis da best dick ya eva had."

"Ouu…yeah. Ouu this feels good. Fuck me Baby. Oou!"

"Wait!" Anthony said. "Turn ova on ya back. Yeah. Slide up on da bed. Ya no wat I wanna do befor I cum" He said.

Neither of them heard the front door open. Usually Anthony double-checked for things like that. He didn't want anyone to walk up on him without him knowing it. Brandi walked down the hall towards the familiar sounds. Her heart beat faster with each step she took. There was no doubt that Anthony was fucking someone but whom? Had he and Jessica gotten back together?

Just as she approached the bedroom door, she heard the other voice and nearly collapsed. "Put my balls in your mouth Anthony."

"Ugh! Son-of-a-bitch!" She screamed. She wanted desperately to turn and run but her feet wouldn't move. She wanted someone to wake her up but her eyes were wide open. Two men. Both of whom she had fucked was in bed together.

"Brandi!" Both men screamed one after the other. Erik tried to cover himself while Anthony jumped up from his knees.

"Dis is not wat ya thin." Anthony responded as he stood there in his nakedness. "I promise ya its not da way it looks."

Chapter 28

"I SHOULD SHOOT BOTH OF YOU BITCHES!" Nikki screamed to the top of her lungs. She entered the bedroom in a rage, knocking over the lamp and swooping everything off the dresser. "YOU MUTHAFUCKAS WANT TO SPOIL SOME SHIT DON'T YOU? OKAY DAMNIT! IT'S SPOILED." Nikki quickly ran out of the bedroom.

Lance and Karen both scrambled to get dressed as they heard Nikki in the kitchen opening drawers. Neither had gotten completely dressed when she returned to the bedroom with a knife. "I'm not going to kill you because I need you but I'm going to teach your damn ass a lesson. Do you think you can go behind my back and spoil shit?" She sprung towards Lance with the knife. He grabbed her hand with the knife in it and put his other arm around her neck.

"Nikki, calm down. We were just fooling around. It means nothing. Take a deep breath and calm down." He told her in a soft but stern voice. "It's going to be alright."

"No it's not!" Nikki began to cry. It's not goanna be alright. You spoiled it. You will pay for this. You spoiled everything! I promise you will pay!"

Karen stood against the wall. She was afraid to move. Was Nikki having some sort of a breakdown? Why the hell was she freaking out? It would be different if she caught Karen with her man but Lance wasn't Nikki's man. Damn!

"I'm fine. Let me go!" Nikki straightened her face and her crying stopped almost as instantly as if had started. "I was just caught off guard. I didn't think we had secrets like that. How long have the two of you been fucking?"

"It's not like that." Karen broke her silence. "Today was the first time. Lance came here looking for you. He didn't come to see me. It just happened."

"It's my fault." Lance told Nikki as he loosened his grip on her. "You can't blame Karen. This one is on me." He looked at Nikki. "Let me have the knife."

She opened her hand and let the knife drop to the floor. Lance kicked the knife in Karen's direction. After Karen secured the knife, Nikki sat on the bed. "I'm sorry for overreacting. I'm going through hell with not being able to see my kids. You have to get them for me soon Lance. Please. Promise me Lance."

"I'll do my best." Lance put his shirt on.

"I think I am going to take a lil nap before I head back to the hotel. I only came back because I left the cell phone here."

"Yeah. That sounds like a good idea. Get you some rest Nikki. You seem to be on overload. I'm going to get up out of here. I have some things to take care of." Lance continued to dress. Afterwards, he walked Nikki to her room and watched her lay down before walking out the door.

Nikki lay quietly in bed. She heard the sound of Lance cranking up his car. "Motherfuckin Bastard!" She mumbled to herself. Slowly she got out of bed and peeked through the window blinds while she watched his car pull out of the driveway and out of sight. She then went to Karen's room where she found Karen on the bed in a near fetal position. She dived on the bed and rolled Karen over before climbing on top of her and choking her.

"Bitch, I will kill your motherfuckin ass if you ever give any more of my fruit away. I'll break your damn neck. This is my damn fruit!"

Karen gasped a couple of times before Nikki released her.

"Nik…ki-" Karen started to plead. Before she could complete her statement, Nikki backhanded her across the face.

"I don't give a fuck about Lance. Damn him. I could care less about a motherfuckin man. Don't I make you feel better than any damn man ever made you feel?"

Karen didn't speak. Nikki slapped her again. "Don't I? Were you enjoying his ass?"

"No Nikki. I wasn't enjoying him. He was enjoying me. He doesn't make me feel like you make feel"

Nikki crawled off Karen and kissed her before lying next to her. She rubbed her face. "Oh Baby. I think you are going to have a nasty bruise there. That's what happens when you spoil things. Why in the fuck do you make me do this shit? Why? Mama only wants to make you feel good. You spoiled it. Promise me you won't do that again." She continued to rub Karen's face. "We're going to have a good time. Soon we'll have another playmate. It'll be Rhonda, you and me. Now apologize to me!"

"I'm sorry Mama. It won't happen again." Karen spoke barely above a whisper.

"I accept your apology. Now take your ass in there and shower so Mama can enjoy some of that juicy fruit. I love you."

If only she knew how much I despise her damn ass. Fuck that crazy bitch. She's just as bad as an abusive man. I will never understand how someone can put their hands on you one minute and expect you to make love to them the next damn minute. That's bullshit! But if I don't there is no telling what that fool will do. The unstable bitch!

Karen stepped into the shower. She made the water as hot as she could stand it without scalding herself. *Damn! I really messed up by getting involved with that bitch. Where the hell did she come from anyway? Why did I cave in like that when I know good and well that I am not gay? Hell, I'd be just as bad as Erik. Yeah Erik. This is his entire damn fault. He didn't have to do me like that. I didn't force him to get involved with me. There are too many damn men out there on the down low. It's because of him that I am in this fucked up situation. Damn bastard.*

Karen let the water run down her body to rinse off. As soon as she turned the shower off and pulled the curtain back, she was face to face with Nikki.

"Let me help you out Baby so I can eat my fruit. Yum…yum."

Chapter 29

Lance looked at his watch. *9:43 a.m. What's taking them so damn long. They are usually out by now. They must be running behind or something.* He had been following Rhonda for quite a while, trying to see if she kept the same schedule. Although her schedule sometimes varied, she never missed bringing her son to this building on Thursday mornings. They were usually in by 8:30 and out by 9:30. He had no ideal of whom they were seeing since the building contained many offices.

He slouched down in the seat of his car; *I've got to do this right. Just the way I planned.* He picked up the ski mask, which was thrown on the passenger seat. *This shit is crazy. I can't drive around town during midmorning with a ski mask on my face. The po-po would surely stop me. But if Rhonda recognizes me I'm sure that bitch will talk. I swear that I can't spend any time locked up.*

Lance looked ahead and saw Rhonda coming out of the building with Nard. *Damn! I don't have a choice. Nikki is crazy. God help me.* He opened the glove compartment and took out the gun. He put it in his pocket and bolted quickly towards Rhonda and Nard.

She was about to put her key in the car to open the door when Lance startled her. "Ma'am, listen up. I have a gun. I don't want to use it but

I will if you make me. I would hate to have to hurt this little kid and I know you don't want to see the lil fella all covered in blood."

"What is it? What do you want?" Rhonda asked. "Money? Please don't hurt us. Take my purse and leave. Just take it." She let her purse drop to the ground.

"Pick up your purse Ma'am. I'm not a robber. I don't want your money. I just need for you to come with me. See that black Ford Explorer right there?"

"I see it." Rhonda held tight to Nard's hand. He didn't understand what was going on. He didn't know they were in danger. She wished he wasn't autistic. If he understood what was happening, she could create a diversion and ask him to run.

"The three of us are going to get in that Explorer and take a little ride. Walk. Go now and nobody will get hurt. Put the lil boy in the front seat with me, and you get in the back. I don't want to hurt anybody."

As they walked towards the Explorer, Rhonda asked, "Why are you doing this?" She turned to look the man in his face for the first time. "Oh my goodness." She put her hands over her mouth. "I know you. I know you from Brooksville. You stood by and watched while Nikki- Oh shit! Nikki. You're doing this for Nikki aren't you? You're the one who helped her escape didn't you? What the hell does Nikki want? I don't have time for this bullshit."

Lance secured Nard in the seatbelt, turned the key in the ignition, put the car in drive and drove away. He tried to block out Rhonda's pleas. He was relieved that at least the child rode quietly. All he did was rock back and forth.

Why don't that woman just shut the hell up? Nikki is not going to hurt them. She wouldn't do anything to hurt her own child. Besides, I have too much to lose if I don't go through with what Nikki wants me to do. She's probably going to flip anyway when she finds out I don't have both kids. It's just best not to cross Nikki. She has some real issues.

"Woman will you shut that trap the hell up? We'll be there soon. The house is only a couple of blocks away. If you stop yapping for a damn minute you will see that I don't mean you any harm."

Lance thought about the fact that he could possibly be charged with kidnapping. "Nikki asked me to pick you up for her. My gun is not even loaded." He lied. "Nikki said you would get a kick out of that. I'm not trying to keep you against your will. You are free to leave at any time. I just don't think you want to go through the hassle with Nikki."

Rhonda wanted to jump out of the car with Nard and run as fast as her feet would carry her. But what good would it do? It would only make Nikki more determined.

"Here we are." Lance told her when he pulled up into Karen's driveway. He was surprised to see the car there. He thought for sure that Nikki would have gotten rid of Karen before he arrived with Rhonda. *Well I guess I shouldn't be surprised. Nikki is always changing the rules in the middle of the game.*

"What's this about? What does Nikki want and how long are we going to have to be here?" Rhonda demanded to know what Nikki had planned. "Tell me man. I have to get back to my daughter."

"I honestly don't know what she wants." He answered. "I guess we will find out soon. Get out."

Nikki opened the door before they reached the steps. It was apparent that she had been anxiously awaiting their arrival. "Where is Dean?" She asked slowly.

"She's with her dad." Rhonda answered. "Nard had an appointment this morning. What the hell do you want Nikki? And what's up with having this man kidnap us at gunpoint?"

"Oh! Is that what he did?" Nikki slapped Lance hard across his face. "You know better than that. you could have hurt somebody."

Lance stood there with a startled look on his face. He had not expected Nikki to slap him, nor was he ready for any kind of confrontation with her. "I apologize." He told Rhonda. "I didn't mean to frighten you."

Nikki concentrated on Nard. "Hello there lil fella."

Nard completely ignored her as he had in the park.

"Do you fuckin hear me talking to you?" she shook Nard.

Rhonda pushed Nikki back. "Keep your damn hands off him and leave him alone. He's autistic. He doesn't know what the hell you are saying."

"You mean he is retarded?" Nikki responded. "He looks normal to me."

"No Nikki, he is not retarded. He has a developmental disorder that affects his expressive and receptive language. He was in speech therapy today before this thug kidnapped us. Now one more time. What are we here for?"

"Lance, stay in here with the kid. Find some cartoons or something for him to watch. Rhonda, you come with me. I have something to show you."

Nikki led her to the next room where Karen lay quietly on the bed naked. She had not changed from the position Nikki put her in. Her legs were spread wide apart and her arms were folded on the pillow behind her head. Rhonda couldn't help but to notice the young Latino beauty with the clean shaven pussy. Rhonda had no idea that Karen kept herself shaven ever since Nikki pulled out patches of her hair. She wondered how the woman had gotten involved with a fugitive.

Nikki suddenly kissed Rhonda while Karen observed in silence. At first, Rhonda tried to turn her head but when Nikki stuck her hand in her pants and started fingering her, she returned the kiss.

"Umph!" Rhonda squealed in a low voice. Nobody had ever worked her pussy like Nikki. She felt good. "Ah…Nikki." She swayed her body.

Nikki stopped. "Get undressed. We can't leave my friend Karen out. After all, this is her house. Do you know how long I have waited to have my cookie and my fruit together?"

Rhonda didn't understand what was coming over her. She despised Nikki but wanted to feel the enjoyment she knew Nikki was about to give her. How the hell could Nikki have such an effect on her?

Bernard fucked her. I'm doing this to get even with his ass. She lied to herself.

Rhonda and Nikki both undressed. Nikki looked at Rhonda. "Get in the bed beside her."

"Karen, I want you to kiss her and then suck her tits while I eat my cookie. Make sure she feels good so she will want to come back to us." Rhonda and Karen kissed. Rhonda could hardly believe what was going down. She didn't even know this woman, yet she was caught up in the excitement like it was the normal thing to do. Nikki spread the lips on her cookie and licked it before gently sucking on her clitoris. She rubbed Rhonda's thighs. "Is this still my cookie?"

"Oh…umph!" Rhonda moaned while Karen was sucking her tits at the same time.

"Damn…that feels so good." She said out loud. "Don't stop. Please don't stop!"

Nikki stopped. "I have to stop. I'm not ready for you to cum yet. Save it. We have to have some fruit. Open your legs Karen."

Karen spread her legs apart again. "Rhonda, show Mama how well you can eat that fruit."

Rhonda slid to the edge of the bed and dove into Karen's fruit. Karen enjoyed the pleasure she was receiving.

"Go ahead." Nikki said. "Eat it! Make her cum. Eat that juicy fruit."

Karen moaned and grabbed Rhonda's hair as she got an orgasm. Nikki, who was fingering herself, got an orgasm right behind Karen. "Oh shit! Oh that feels good!" She screamed.

"What about me?" Rhonda asked. "Am I not going to get mine?"

"Yeah! I gotcha Baby. I love you. Lay back. I have something special for you."

Rhonda slid back to the center of the bed. Nikki walked over to the dresser drawer and strapped up. She then placed a French tickler condom on the strap-on and inserted it in Rhonda. "Oh my good... ness."

Karen sucked Rhonda's breast while she lay there moving her body to catch each stroke Nikki threw at her.

"YEAH!" Rhonda screamed. "Ah...ah...! Da...am!" She screamed louder.

Nikki pulled out of Rhonda and got off the bed. "What the hell are you doing Nikki? Damn! Why do you always do that?"

"Wait." Nikki answered. She opened the drawer next to the bed and pulled out a glass dick. "This is what I have been saving for you. This is what Mama wants to put up in the sweet cookie." She fucked Rhonda with the glass dick while Karen licked her body. Rhonda rotated her body and moaned as she enjoyed the feeling that was traveling through her body.

They all looked towards the direction of the door when they heard a noise. Lance had left Nard in the other room and was standing in the doorway. His pants were dropped to his ankles and he was jacking his dick while he let out sounds resembling a sick patient in pain.

"Let me put it in." He begged while continuing to jack his dick.

"No!" Nikki answered. "You would only spoil it." She continued to fuck Rhonda with the glass dick. Rhonda's body shook from the orgasm.

Lance let out a loud "Augh…augh… augh… um… that's…it!" He spilled his juices on the bedroom floor.

Chapter 30

"You sick motherfuckers. You sick twisted ass motherfuckers. You on your fuckin knees between Erik's legs and you tell me it is not what the hell I think? You disgust me."

"Brandi, I'm sorry. I never wanted you to-" Erik didn't finish his sentence.

"Stop!" Brandi put her hand up. "Don't say shit to me Erik. Anthony is probably new to the game. But not you. You have been getting your dick sucked for a while."

Brandi had dated Erik briefly while Anthony was in prison. One evening she had gone to his office after hours and found him standing with his male P.A. sucking his dick. She was distraught and literally threw up in the floor.

Anthony walked towards Brandi. "Let's talk gurl. I need ta esplain thins ta ya."

"You don't have to explain shit to me. Fuck you Anthony. I don't need you. What the hell you need to do is be true to your damn self."

She turned to leave and Anthony grabbed her arm. "Erik, lemme talk ta Brandi fer a minute. Please man, I don wan hur ta leave dis way."

"Don't fuckin touch me, you could have told me that your ass was on the fucking down low. You didn't have to waste my time. There is nothing I can do for you. Not one fuckin thing!" Brandi screamed.

Erik got dressed to leave. When he reached the doorway, he stopped and looked at Brandi. "I'm really sorry Brandi. I never meant to hurt you." He then turned to Anthony. "I'll talk to you later Anthony." When Erik nodded his head, he walked out the door.

"Just gimme ten minutes Brandi. Dats all I ask. Ten minutes and I won bother ya no mo. Please Brandi."

She sat on the wing back chair in the far corner of the room. "Talk Anthony. Go ahead and talk but I don't have anything to say."

"I dint wanna hurt ya. I really dint but ya kept on comin round. I don changed. I'm not dat same ole Ant ya use ta no. Prison don change me. Some peeps say it don change ya but ya hafta be a strong muthafucka fer it not ta change ya. Ya don no what I been thru." He turned his head.

"What about me Anthony? Am I supposed to pay for what you went through?

"No Brandi. But-"

"That's my fault. I should have known. I heard people say that men get turned out when they go to prison. I heard that they end up in the cell with a Big Bubba and get raped." Tears rolled down her cheeks.

"No Brandi. Dat shit aint true. Everybody dat go in don get fucked. Peeps say dat shit but it aint like dat. In fact ya get mo time if ya rape sumbody in prison. Its just dat da man dey put me in da cell with had life. He dint have nunthin ta lose. He was termined not ta spen da rest of his life jackin his dick."

"So what did he do to you?" Brandi looked at him.

"I wuz young wen I got put in dat fuckin hell hole. I wuz scared and he wuz big as hell. Da first nite I wuz der, and da lights went out he pulled his big black dick out and told me ta suck it. I said no but he grabbed my head and said, *Suck my muthafuckin dick and if you bite me I will kill your ass.*"

Anthony spoke softly. Brandi could see that he was getting emotional. "I took his dick in my mouf and tried ta suck it. I wuz nervous. I dint wan ta hurt it. Afta bout five minutes he told me ta just take my ass on ta bed."

He walked over to the window and looked through the blinds as he continued to tell Brandi his story. "Da next nite he told me dat I wuz goanna fuck him. I wuz real nervous. My dick wuz not even hard. So he sucked me and ta my surprise it felt gud. I don know if I wuz just missin ya or wat but it felt gud and my dick got hard as hell. He put a lota lotion on my dick and den he bent ova. I stuck my dick in his ass and his ass wuz warm. I closed my eyes and imagined I wuz goin deep in ya Brandi. And I fucked him til we bof came."

Brandi put her hand over her chest. She was getting choked up as she tried to keep from crying. "Oh my goodness Anthony."

"He wuz a big man but he wuz really a kitten. He neva fucked me. I always fucked him. He taught me wat ta do and I enjoyed it."

Brandi cleared her throat. "What about me? Why didn't you tell me you were like that? Why didn't you say you were gay? I am so sick of these men being on the DL and bringing innocent women into their web of deceit. If it's something that you are ashamed of then simply don't do it. And if you choose to do it, then don't be ashamed."

"Brandi, ya just don understan.

"No Anthony. I don't understand. I don't understand how you ended up with Erik. Was this your way of getting back at me for fucking Erik while you were in prison?"

"What? Ya just telling a damn lie. Erik neva fucked ya." He protested.

"I have no reason to lie to you Anthony honey. I see that while he was satisfied with laying back having you suck his dick that he failed to tell you about us. It's ironic that you ended up with him after he tried his best to convince me that you were nothing but a loser. He told me several times to get rid of your ass. The two of you are now sucking each other's dick, and Heaven knows what else. You guys deserve each other." She cried.

"Brandi, I'm sorry. Dats all I can say. Erik was an accident. Just like ya being here wen da po-po came wuz an accident. I don wanna cause ya no trouble. I'm goanna take care of dat fer ya."

"You fucked up my reputation and everything. I have a damn job. I could lose my job behind this bullshit and I haven't done a damn thing. I didn't know there were drugs in this house."

Anthony walked to her. "Its gon be fine. Erik is gon- I mean I'm gon take care of everthin."

"Nah! I heard you." Brandi raised her voice. "You were about to say Erik is going to take care of everything. That's what you were about to say. Are you selling drugs for Erik? Is he your supplier, or connection, or whatever it is you call the big man?"

Anthony placed his hands on her shoulders. "Calm down."

"Calm down my ass!" You are stupid. Stupid as hell. Erik is using your black ass to suck his dick and make his money. He doesn't give a damn about you. You're just his flunky." She removed his hands from her shoulders. "Get your damn hands off me."

"Ya don know wat ya talking bout." He told her.

"You'll see." Brandi told him. "And it's going to be a sad day when you end up back in prison. I'm not doing it." She walked out slamming the door behind her.

Chapter 31

Anthony thought long and hard about what Brandi had said. Could it be possible that Erik was using him? Thinkin back on da big picture, he was the one takin all the risks. He was the one who dealt wit all the contacts and who put da boys on the streets. Erik was kindly tucked away in his mansion with his nice doctors' salary. And why da hell dint Erik never mentioned bout him and Brandi had been kickin it?

Anthony wondered if he had made a mistake. He faced possibly going to prison again. Before now, he had been prepared to do anything he needed to do in order to keep Erik's secret. Now that Brandi had thrown those words out there, he began to wonder. He wasn't sure any more. Anthony picked up the phone. After dialing five numbers, he pushed the *end* button.

What da hell am I goin ta say? What if Brandi is right? I love him. Why did he let me love him? Anthony picked the telephone up again. He dialed Erik's number. "Watsup? She's gud. Ima be needin ta talk ta ya. Can ya come bak ova or can we meet sum where?"

Anthony was not allowed to come to Erik's house. That had been understood from the beginning. Erik would come to him. It would usually be late at night

"Nah man. It's important. Dis can't wait. Ima need ta see ya tunite." Anthony wanted to resolve the situation as soon as possible. He felt that as soon as he talked to Erik face to face, he'd be able to figure out his next move.

"Okay. Ima be waitin rite here."

Anthony hung up the telephone and walked to his bedroom. He sat on the bed and thought. *I hope dat Brandi is wrong. I no dat dis muthafucka ain't tryna make no fool outta me. He betta know who he dealin wit. Brandi probably just jealous. I shuda told her. I no she hurt but I'm not da man she usta no. I just hope she wrong bout Erik. I don no wat ta think.*

Anthony stood up and walked to the living room. He admired his nice house and furniture. He couldn't have any of that without Erik. He didn't want to lose his nice house and cars. Why hadn't he stopped while he was ahead of the game? What was it about that fast money that made you crave more of it? The more you made, the more you wanted to make. Eventually you think you know the game and you are above the law. Then your world comes crashing down on you. Once that happens, you risk losing it all; including your freedom.

The headlights beamed through the living room curtains as Erik pulled into the driveway. Anthony quickly opened the door and stood in the doorway until Erik walked up on the porch. "Come in." He told Erik as he opened the door and stood aside.

"Anthony, what the hell is going on? You sounded rather anxious over the telephone. Is there anything wrong?" He questioned.

"Come in an hab a seat. I wanna talk a ya bout sumthin." Anthony walked to the bar and fixed himself a drink. "Wan one?" He held up his glass to Erik.

"Yes." Erik answered. "Grey Goose on the rocks. What do we need to talk about? Spit it out. I was busy when you called."

"Man, why in da hell ain't ya tell me ya wuz da one fuckin Brandi when I wuz in? Wat up wit dat shit? Wat ya doin? Is ya playin sum kinda game or sumthin?" He looked at Erik awaiting a response. Erik was silent. "Talk ta me man."

"Anthony, the thing with Brandi only happened because of her need and because of my being a friend. I'm not interested in women and you know that. Brandi knows that also. No doubt, she sought a relationship but I can't let her turn me into something that I am not." Erik took a sip of his drink. "Have a seat and let me talk to you about something while I am here."

"Okay Erik. I'm listnin. Wat otha shock ya got in store fer me?"

"No shock. I think you know how this works. They are going to try to make a deal with you. That's just the way they do. They will ask you to roll over on your connection in return for a deal. The deal is not actually a deal but the same amount of time that you would in other words get. It is no sentence reduction. I know you would never put me out there like that." Erik stood. "I don't think you will have to do a bid Anthony but if it does come down to that, I will be more valuable to you on the outside than I would be on the inside."

Anthony pondered over what Erik had said. "So tell me man. Wat da hell are ya sayin? Sounds like ya throwin me out dere man. I don wanna do no mo dam time. Dat shit ain't no fuckin picknick." He responded. "I can't go bak in dat dam place."

Erik strolled over to where Anthony was and took his hand. "Anthony, hopefully it won't come to that. I have every reason to believe that you will come out of this mess on top. Trust me. You have the best lawyer in the region. I'm just speaking of worse case scenario and I'm saying that the D.A. will try to intimidate you into giving up your supplier. These people don't play fair. If you talk, your life won't be worth three cents, I am not threatening you. I am not talking about from me. This shit is so damn much bigger than me. You have to trust me!" He exclaimed.

Anthony noticed the look of concern on Erik's face. Maybe Brandi was wrong. He cudn't thro Erik out dere. Not witout getting others involved. He had to protect himself. Besides, it was not like they could prove da drugs belong to him. A lot of people had come in an out of his house. He aint sold drugs to no undercover agent or anything like that. In fact, he was not even on the streets. Redd was in charge of handlin the runners. Redd was his right hand man and they had not picked Redd up so he shud be just fine.

"What are you thinking?" Erik questioned.

"Nunthin really." He answered. "Jus thin dat wen I get outta dis shit, Ima chill fer a while. Wata bout ya.? Is we gon be tagatha or wat? I'm tired of all dis damn hiden. Dis ain't fair. We is bof grown. Ya ain't even never let me come ta ya house cause ya so scared." Anthony had kept his concerns to himself for long enough. "Dis shit ain't fair. Society wana put all dis shit out dere ta make us look like we freaks or sumthin and den got us hidin ta keep people from talkin. Dam dem people."

Erik glanced at him not quite knowing what to say. He had deliberately kept Anthony away from his house. Anthony was not his man. He was just a playmate whom served the purpose of a good fringe benefit. By sexing Anthony, he was able to keep him where he wanted him and continue to use him for the business. Maybe he should have kept sex out of the equation with Anthony but he had to gain Anthony's trust. His real man and his lover was his P.A. and there was no way he'd ever leave his lover for a ex-convict whom had recently gotten his G.E.D. but had the vocabulary of an illiterate adult. No way. Although he had to admit the man was street smart, and that's what he had needed to get things up and running.

He snickered. "Come on now dude. You know that I live in an upscale neighborhood with nosey ass neighbors. If a black man were seen coming in and out of my residence, it would raise all kinds of questions. It's not that you are not welcome because you are. We have our own private lil getaway. Let's just keep things the way they are for the time being. Don't worry. Things are going to work out just fine."

Anthony had a woeful look on his face as he walked to the door. He placed his hand on the doorknob and opened the door. "Ya can lev man. I just hope ya ain't tryna play me." He whispered.

Erik strolled towards the door. "Don't I get a kiss before I leave?"

After Anthony closed the door, the two men lip-locked. "I'll see you soon." Erik told him before opening the door. "Don't worry. It's all going to work out."

"It betta!" He mumbled. "I'm not tryna do no mo time."

Chapter 32

Rhonda was relieved to be home. Nard was unaware of the events that had transpired throughout the day. Bernard's car was not home so he was obviously out with Dean. That was good. It allowed her time to get her thoughts together. What a wild ass play time. Karen seemed to be a little nervous at first. *I can teach her a few things*. Rhonda thought. *I can tell that she is not use to freakin.*

Nard sat on the floor with the television remote control in his hand. He switched between the animal channel and the music channel. Rhonda wondered if he would outgrow his diagnoses. Would he one day be a productive citizen in society? She had not gotten as much information on autism as she should have. With Bernard being an exceptional children's teacher, he should have known how to best deal with the situation.

Rhonda paced the floor recalling how fulfilled she had felt when she left Karen's. This hadn't been what she wanted. How had she let herself get caught up in the moment? Why had she allowed herself to be pleased? That was crazy. She knew that Nikki was unstable. The bitch was capable of all sorts of things. So why in the hell was it so enjoyable? Why did her mind keep bouncing back to Karen? Nikki was the one calling the shots. Rhonda wondered how Karen had been sucked into

Nikki's web. The psycho was like that. She had a way of manipulating people and getting them to do exactly what she wanted them to do.

"Eeee…eee!" Nard let out a loud shriek and covered his ears. He got on the couch and covered his ears with both hands.

"What's wrong Baby?" Rhonda's thoughts switched from Karen to Nard. Why was he making that loud noise and covering his ears? Was he hurt? Did he have a earache? Had he stuck something in his ears? Rhonda was nervous and worried. She picked up the telephone to call her husband. She had just hit the speed dial button when she heard the keys in the front door and Dean came running in.

"Hey Mama we had fun. We went out to eat after we left the park and plus I had chocolate ice cream." She ran to where Nard sat rocking in the chair. Dean pulled his hands from his ears to kiss him but each time he put them back.

"Leave him alone Sweetie. I think he has an ear infection."

"Who has as ear infection?" Bernard questioned while walking into the room.

"Nard." She answered. "He suddenly started making noises and holding his ears. I don't know what else could be wrong." Rhonda responded.

"I think I know. He'll be fine." Bernard told her. "Yesterday I noticed that the Martin's have gotten a puppy. It was barking when I pulled into the driveway. Most autistic children get upset at the sound of a dog barking. It irritates them. I bet that's what has Nard so upset. He is making that noise to drown out the sound of the barking dog. That's why he has his ears covered Sweetness. He'll take his hands down after a while. How did everything go today? Dean and I waited but the two of you took so long that we figured the session had gone into overtime." Bernard said.

"No!" Rhonda answered. "It didn't go into overtime. When the session was over, I decided to just hang out with Nard for a while. I pointed out some things to him and named them. I would point to a tree and say tr…ee. I pointed to a window and said win…dow. Things like that. I am just trying to help build his vocabulary."

She hated to lie on Nard but there was no way she could tell Bernard that she had been laid up in bed enjoying Nikki and another woman while Nard played in the other room. Although, from past experiences, she wondered if he really would have minded. Who knows? He probably would have wanted to get in on the action with his magic stick. It seemed lately that one pussy was not enough to satisfy him.

Baby, you are going to have to get more information on autism. Nard is going to be fine. I don't want him to be autistic any more than you do but it is what it is. You taking him outside and sounding out trees and windows is just not going to get it. I know that you had the best intentions in the world. Things are going to have to be structured for him. He has two loving parents so he will learn. Failure is not an option." Bernard spoke positively.

Two loving parents. I wonder if Nikki will ever get herself together and come for the kids. I wonder if she will give us trouble later on down the road. Rhonda was in such deep thought; she had drowned her husband out.

"Rhonda!" Bernard raised his voice. "Where did you go? Did you not hear me talking to you? I was asking if you'd like a break today. I thought you might want to go out tonight."

"Well it really would be nice to have a break but let's stay in. I don't feel like getting dressed to go out. How about if we just order pizza?" She asked. "We can pop in a movie for Dean and let Nard play with his legos."

"Okay. That'll work. I'll call in the pizza. Let me shower and get comfortable. We'll relax tonight." He replied.

That sounded great to Rhonda whom hadn't quite gotten over her earlier escapade. For some reason, she found it difficult to get Karen off her mind. Nikki must have something on Karen. But what? Rhonda didn't know but she intended to find out.

Nard finally removed his hands from his ears. Rhonda noticed that the dog had stopped barking. She knew that she had a lot to learn about autism. Maybe she'd try to get into some workshops or seminars on autism.

Dean was such a trooper. She accepted her brother and was patient with him, whenever Nard wanted something and pointed to it, she would sound out the word. *Po-ta-to Ch-ips. Is that what you want? Say it. Po-ta-to Ch-ips.* Nard would only be able to say part of the word but he'd try even though he would continue to point. *Ta-chi.* Dean would always smile and tell him he did a good job before she gave him what he wanted.

Rhonda wondered if her husband had accepted Nard and his disability. She noticed he didn't spend as much time with Nard as he did with Dean. If she decided to separate from him, she would keep both kids with her. After today, she couldn't be sure what she wanted. All she knew at the moment was that things didn't look good for Bernard.

Chapter 33

Anthony wondered why in the hell the D.A. wanted to talk to him. Hadn't they done enough when they kicked his door in? What were they going to do to him next? Serve him with another warrant? He knocked on the door that said District Attorney. "Come in." A voice from the other side of the door called out.

Anthony opened the door and walked in. The D.A. asked him to have a seat. "Anthony, I asked you to come here so I can help you."

"Nah man! Com on now. Who ya thin ya talkin ta? Miss me wit dat shit. I don belibe ya. Why ya wanna help me?" Anthony stood to leave. "Ya wasted my time comin here fer dat shit."

"If you walk out that door without listening to me, you will be making the biggest mistake of your life." He said to Anthony.

With what seemed a mighty effort, Anthony sat back down in the seat. "Talk. Ya got ten minutes and den Ima walk out dat door."

The District Attorney looked Anthony in his eyes. "You are facing some serious prison time. I won't lie to you. I know that you aren't the mastermind behind this drug ring. There is someone higher up than you. You're only a flunky. I want the big man. Or are you willing to go down for him?"

As he sat quietly in the chair, Anthony recalled the words Brandi had said to him. *But dere is no way Erik wud let him go bak to prison. He cud not subvibe in there a second time.*

The District Attorney continued. "We've had your house under observation for quite a while prior to executing the search warrant. You've made a lot of money selling cocaine. Who is your supplier?"

Anthony squirmed in his seat. There was a tap at the door before a man walked in and sat in the chair next to Anthony. He extended his hand to Anthony.

"Hi. I'm Detective Todd Foster. I'll cut through the chase. I don't believe in dragging things out and I don't believe in begging. The D.A. wants to work with you. He wants to give you a chance. He believes in getting the big fish. I believe there are a lot of small fish out there and if you catch enough of them, they'll make as much of a meal as one big fish."

Anthony was quiet. He could hear his heart beating and feel it break dancing in his chest. He didn't like the smart-ass detective. *Dis bastard acts like his ass jus wanna unlock da damn dor, throw my ass in der head first and den jus swallow da muthafuckin key.* Anthony thought to himself. *I'm not feelin dis muthafucka at tall.* He stood again.

"I'm outta here."

"Go on." Detective Foster replied as he stepped aside to allow room for Anthony to exit. "Go on but I know that you have massed a small fortune in cash money related to your cocaine distribution business. Your truck driving is only a front to help you explain having a house, cars, money and all that cash. You won't need any of that where you're going. Bye! Get out!" He exclaimed.

Without another word, Anthony walked out the door and down the hall. He wished he had not bothered to show up. Now he was confused. *Dat muthafucka talked ta me like I wuz a damn dummy. I know what he thin. He thin I'm a snitch. Erik ain't gon let me go bak in dere. Is he? Nah! He wudn't do dat. He paid my bond. He ain't gon let me do anutha bid. I don care wat dat damn Foster said and I don care wat Brandi said. Dey don no him like I do.* Anthony concluded.

He got in his car and decided to drive to Brandi's house. He felt like she was still upset with him since she hadn't called. Brandi had always been fair however and he still considered her a friend. A friend is what he needed now. It would be great if he could go to Erik's office and talk to him but that was forbidden.

Anthony remembered the one and only time he had gone to Erik's office. He had signed in at the window. "Do you have an appointment Sir?" I don't see your name on the list. It's fine. I'll just pull your file." The receptionist had stated.

"Nah! I don got no apponment. I jus need ta see da doc. It's impordant. Tell em dat Antonee is here. He'll see me."

"Have a seat please. He's with a patient at the moment." She had looked at him like he was some sort of homeless pill head seeking Erik to beg for a prescription or something.

He sat down and observed as she whispered to one of the nurses. The nurse then looked at him, doing everything in her power to be discreet but it was obvious to him that they had been talking about him. Who the hell did they think he was any damn way? He was dressed decently. Did they think he couldn't afford a doctor or what? He waited for about twenty minutes before Erik came out.

"May I help you Sir?"

"Sir? Sir?" Anthony chuckled. "Weere da hell dis Sir stuff come from?"

"Mister, if you need to be seen, you will have to make an appointment. I don't take walk-ins. If you have an emergency, you will need to go to the hospital. Now, if you will excuse me, I have patients to see." Erik walked away.

Anthony was left in the waiting room feeling like a complete fool. He walked to the elevator wondering what had happened. When he got in his car and pulled out of the parking lot, his cell phone rang. He saw that Erik was calling.

"What the fuck was that?" Erik had asked without giving him the chance to say anything. "My office is off limits. Don't ever do that shit again. When I am at work, I am a professional." Having said all that he wanted to say, Erik had hung up the telephone. Anthony was left feeling cheap and abandoned.

Later that night when Erik called, Anthony had thought it was to apologize. Instead, Erik had continued to reprimand him. "What the hell were you thinking anyway? What did you expect me to do? Don't you understand my position? I have a reputation to uphold in this city."

"I no ya do." Anthony stated. "Damn man. Ya ack like I wuz gon come in der and tongue ya down in front of people. I came by ta see if ya mite wanna git away fer sum lunch or sumthin." He had tried to defend his actions but since Erik wasn't hearing it, he decided to give up trying.

Erik seemed to hold the grudge for a while. It was about two weeks before Anthony heard anything from him. When he did finally hear from Erik, he was so thrilled to be with his lover that he dared not mention the unannounced visit.

Brandi had barely pulled into her driveway when Anthony pulled in behind her. She stepped out of the car. "What do you want Anthony?"

"I just wanna talk. Can I come in? Please Brandi?" He begged.

"We don't have anything to talk about. I don't know why you're here. Just leave me alone." She turned to walk towards her porch.

"Brandi, don do dis gurl. I jus need ta talk ta ya fer ten minutes and den I'll lev."

"Come on in Anthony." Brandi looked through her keys until she found the one that unlocked the front door. She unlocked the door and dropped her purse on the couch. "Have a seat. What do you want Anthony?" She asked without seeming the least bit interested.

Anthony sat in the middle of the couch. He placed one hand in the other and started wringing his hands together before he spoke. "I jus come bak from dat ass D.A.'s office."

"And what happened Anthony? Why were you there?" Brandi asked suddenly interested.

"Dem muthafuckas wan me ta turn States ebedence and roll ova on my contact. Dey fulla shit Brandi. I thin dat detectiff tryna scare me." He stated.

"That's what they do Anthony. It is part of their job. But how can you take your ass back to prison and chill knowing that your lover is out here with his dick up another man's ass? Answer that one for me. It sounds crazy as hell to me. I know you can't be that stupid. Why the hell are you wasting my time with this shit. It's between Erik and you like everything else is between Erik and you." Brandi sashayed to the kitchen and opened the refrigerator. "Would you like something to drink?"

"Nah! I don wan nunthin ta drink. From da way ya actin. I guess I shudna come here but I thot ya wud help me out. I thot we cud at lest still be friends." He murmured.

"Help you?" Brandi shouted. "Help you and be friends. Wow!" She began to cackle. "What damn world are you living in? You're a joke Anthony. A lying ass joke. You played me. I don't want to be your damn friend. Whatever the hell happens to you it will be what you deserve." She walked to the door and opened it. "Your time is up. Get the hell out of my damn house."

Anthony stood. He reached for Brandi who threw both hands in the air and stepped back.

"OUT!" She screamed.

He walked out the door without closing it behind him. When he was on the porch, he slowly turned towards the door where Brandi stood with tears in her eyes. He wanted to say something to her. He wanted to tell her how sorry he was but the look on her face told him that she wasn't ready to listen. He turned away and headed to his car. He'd have to figure this thing out on his own.

Chapter 34

Lance smiled as he recalled the ordeal at Karen's house. *That's the best damn nut I've busted in a long time.* He thought. It had excited the hell out of him to see the women engaged in pleasing one another. They were so deep into it. He noticed how Nikki seemed to enjoy women more than she enjoyed him. Even when they were with Karen it was as if he were just along from the ride.

As he pulled in front of Karen's house he couldn't help but to wonder if Nikki had just used him all along. She was always making threats and ordering him around. Still, he didn't feel like she was one he could cross. He knew he had made a mistake by getting involved with her. Hopefully that mistake wouldn't come back to bite him in the ass.

Before Lance could ring the doorbell, the door flew open. "Hurry up and get your ass in here. What took you so damn long? You know how I feel about waiting." Nikki scolded.

"I'm sorry. My wife had an appointment. I got here as fast as I could." He responded softly while looking down at the floor.

Without warning, Nikki slapped him hard across the face. "Don't tell me shit about your wife having an appointment. Damn your fuckin wife. When I tell you that I need to see your ass right away, that's what the hell I mean. RIGHT AWAY!" She screamed.

Lance was speechless. *How the hell can she expect me to jump every damn time she whimpers. She knew I had a damn wife when she got involved with me. I don't believe in hitting a woman but if that crazy bitch put her hands in my face one more damn time, I'm going to have to show her ass just how much of a man I really am.* "What the hell did you do that for?" He managed to ask.

"What the hell did you do that for? What the hell did you do that for?" She said in a babyish voice, mimicking Lance. "Don't question me about any damn thing I do muthafucka." She said in a deeper harsher voice. "I run this shit."

Karen walked into the room. "Hey Lance. I didn't hear the door. How are you?" She asked politely.

"I'm good." He answered rolling his eyes at Nikki. "So what's up Nikki? What do you need?"

"Have a seat. You too Karen." She snickered.

Karen flinched as she took a seat next to Lance. She had lost sleep so many nights wondering how she was stupid enough to let Nikki con her. And that's exactly how she felt. Like she had been conned. Nikki knew that Karen was vulnerable and she took advantage of it. Now Karen was trapped. Not only had she had an affair with a patient who was mentally unstable but also she had aided that same patient in escaping from a mental facility. She felt like a slave on the plantation scared to do anything that would upset her Master.

Nikki walked over to where the two sat. "Y'all know that damn Bernard is taking advantage of my friend Rhonda. He has her feeling sorry for his no good ass and acting like he loves her so fuckin much that he can't live without her. She is not happy!" Nikki slammed her fist on the coffee table.

"What do you want us to do about it?" Lance asked even though he wasn't quite sure if he was ready to hear the answer or not.

"I need more time. Lance, I need for you to get close to Bernard or meet him at the bar and befriend him or something. Anything. As long as you can occupy him for a few hours so he doesn't come home. Karen, you are going to have to watch the kids. You and I will figure out how we are going to do this and what to say, once Lance has Bernard occupied." She looked at the two for a response.

Karen sat speechless. What was there to say? Nikki was running the show. Lance broke the silence by responding. "I hope you don't expect all of this to happen right away. I can't gain the man's trust overnight."

"Shut the hell up Lance." She looked at Karen. "I've got it. The perfect plan."

"What Nikki?" Karen asked.

"Rhonda said something about hiring a part-time Nanny to help with the kids. You are going to apply for that position. She'll hire you because she has met you and it seems to me that she likes you. That's it. You are going over there TO…DAY!" Nikki sounded proud of herself for coming up with that plan.

Karen knew it would be pointless to argue with Nikki. She loved children and she could use the extra money even though she was not sure about Nikki's motives. She didn't know what Nikki was up to but she knew that she didn't want to be a part of it. She held her head down.

"Hold your damn head up. Did you hear what I said?" Nikki raised her voice.

"Yes Nikki, I heard you." Karen slowly raised her head. "What do you want me to say? Nothing is going to make you change your mind. You come up with these ideas and you expect Lance and me to abide. I'll go to Rhonda's as soon as I shower and dress." She headed to her room.

"Wait a damn minute." Nikki exclaimed. "Did you call yourself being smart? Is that what that lil speech was about?"

Before she could respond, Lance stood. "I didn't take it that way Nikki. I don't think she was trying to be smart. She was just saying that we are always doing whatever you ask without question or hesitation."

"Yeah. That's exactly what I was saying." Karen chimed in. She went to her bedroom. She was not prepared to battle with Nikki about something so simple. She could apply for the nanny job and pray that she got hired. That would at least allow her to be rid of Nikki a few hours a day. Come to think of it, this job might not be such a bad idea after all. She gathered her things and went in the bathroom to shower.

****

When Karen arrived at Rhonda's house she felt slightly nervous. She had not seen Rhonda since the episode in her bedroom. She rang the doorbell. A voice over the intercom speaker asked, "Yes? May I help you?"

"Hi. I don't know if you remember me or not. It's Karen. I've come to apply for the Nanny position."

"Oh. I'm sorry." Rhonda answered. "I had taken a nap and enabled the alarm. Wait for the green light and then open the door."

When Karen entered the foyer, Rhonda was standing there in shorts and a tank top. "Come in Karen. Of course I remember you. That day wasn't one to easily forget. So you want to apply for the Nanny job huh? Well how did you hear about the job?"

She hesitated before answering. "Well to be honest with you, Nikki mentioned it to me. I love children and I could use the extra money."

"Did Nikki put you up to applying for this job?" Rhonda questioned.

Karen sat on the couch. "May I be completely honest with you Rhonda?" She asked.

"Sure. Go ahead."

"Nikki was instrumental in getting me to apply for this position but I need it. Not only can I use the extra money but it will allow me to have some time away from her. I know that she is your friend but she's peculiar and I need a break from her."

Rhonda sighed. "Nah! Not peculiar. She's crazy as hell. I know. And I wouldn't exactly call Nikki my friend. If you don't mind me asking, how did you get involved with her?"

"It's a long story." Her facial expression showed signs of shame. "It was stupid and it never should have happened. She caught me at a time when I was going through some things. I would like to say she took advantage of me but looking back on it, I should have known better. Now, I'm in over my head, aiding an escaped felon." Tears rolled down her cheeks.

"It's okay." Rhonda told her. "Been there, done that. I know how easy it is to get caught up in Nikki's web. She's not like the rest of us. She doesn't have a conscience."

Karen wondered how Rhonda had gotten caught up. She decided not to ask. It seemed that they had both gone through their own private hell with the bitch. Her thoughts were interrupted when Rhonda spoke.

"If you really want the job, it's yours. It's only part-time. Dean is very talkative once she gets to know you. You have already met Nard so you know he is autistic. They are both great kids Nard has a habit of pointing to things he wants. We don't feed into that unless he makes an effort to say the word. If he points to chips, you will say the word. Ch-ips. If he doesn't say it, you will repeat the word and follow it up with a question. Do you want ch-ips? Ch-ips. Usually he will then attempt to repeat the word. At that point you would give him the chips."

Karen nodded. "Thanks. When do I start?"

"Well the kids will be home soon and so will my husband Bernard. If you'd like to stay for dinner, we are having pork chops, baked potatoes, tossed salad and garlic bread. You can meet everybody tonight and start work tomorrow if you'd like."

"That'll be great." Karen answered. She wondered what Rhonda's husband was like. He obviously wasn't satisfying her if she had gotten involved with Nikki's looney ass.

"Come on then. Why are you sitting there? Help me with dinner." She led Karen to the kitchen. "It's going to be nice having you."

Chapter 35

Lance walked into Brooksville and headed in the direction of the crowd. He wondered what was going on. "What's up?" He asked.

"We were just discussing that damn Nicole Harris. They had her face on the newscast a while ago. Nobody can figure out how she escaped. The investigators were questioning Mrs. Covington." One of the nurses answered.

"They should know that Mrs. Covington didn't have anything to do with that shit." Another nurse added.

"But wonder where she is? She couldn't have got far with no money and no transportation. I thought for sure they would have caught her by now. What do you think Lance? You worked that night didn't you? Did anything seem out of the ordinary?" Someone asked."

"I vaguely remember that night. I did work that night but I think I was just about to get off when they discovered she was gone. I believe that Mrs. Covington worked that zone."

"Oh hell." One of the nurses said. "That explains it. That's why no one knew she was missing all night. Don't yall remember? When first shift came in and the police were swarming this place, Mrs. Covington was not here. They said she left in a hurry because her daughter had been rushed to the hospital. Didn't she get beat up or something?"

Lance listened to the women talk without responding. He felt bad about the situation. Mrs. Covington was a sweet woman and he didn't want her to get in trouble or be investigated for something he was responsible for doing. His mind wandered as he contemplated a way to help her. The police were making a colossal mistake if they were looking in her direction.

"Poor Mrs. Covington. She needs this job. I hope she doesn't get fired behind that crazy ass woman. You know she be trying to take care of them grandkids. Her daughter is strung out on drugs." An elderly woman responded.

"Yeah but I heard that her other daughter is moving back from Texas. She and her husband are well off. I think they will take the kids if they can get custody."

"Excuse me Ladies." Lance said. "I need to get to work. He signed in and began to check on his patients. As he approached room #341 he hesitated. Although Nikki gave Mildred a hard time, the patient seemed to miss her. He prayed they would find another roommate for her soon.

If only I could turn back the hands of time. Nikki would have her black ass right here in room #341 with Mildred. Sooner or later the authorities are going to catch up with her and I certainly don't trust her ass not to throw me under the bus. Once they question her about how she was able to escape she'll boast about how she was clever enough to coax me into helping her. Either that, or the fool will play the role of the victim and claim that I raped her and she escaped out of fear. I don't put anything past that woman.

Lance remembered hearing one of the women say something about them offering a reward for information that would lead to the arrest and conviction of Nikki. If he could turn her in without implicating himself, he'd do it in a heartbeat. But what if he tried and failed? What if Nikki found out? He knew the answer as soon as the thought cleared his mind. Nikki would kill him. She would not hesitate to kill his ass.

Chapter 36

Karen was excited to be starting her part-time job. She arrived an hour and a half early so she could talk with Rhonda and get any instructions she may need. Bernard had left that morning for a school conference out of town.

"There is not really much to tell. You will learn as you go." Rhonda told her. "It'll be another hour before the kids get here. They like you though. Dean was impressed with you last night."

"She is a lovely child." Karen responded. "I really admire the way she looks after her brother."

"Yeah. That's my lil sidekick. Look, I am going to only be out for a couple of hours. I'm going to hang out with my friend Brandi for a while. She seems to be going through something."

Karen sat. "I'm sorry to hear that. Hopefully things will work out for her." Karen stated.

"Hopefully. I'm going to jump in the shower quickly and then I will answer any questions you have." Rhonda told her before prancing up the stairs. She lathered her body down and enjoyed a relaxing shower. The steam filled the bathroom and the hot water felt good running down her body. It felt good to shower every once in a while. The majority of the time, she relaxed in the Jacuzzi in the middle of the bathroom adjacent to her bedroom.

Rhonda pulled the shower curtains back and stuck her hand out to grab the towel off the rack. When she didn't feel a towel she stepped out questioning herself as to whether or not she had taken a towel from the linen closet. As she exited the bathroom naked, Nikki appeared in the doorway.

"You scared me. What the hell are you doing here? How did you get in?" Rhonda asked.

"I rang the doorbell and Karen let me in. She didn't want to." Nikki snickered. "But I told her if she didn't. I'd break out every window in the house. All I want is to check on my cookie. Is my cookie okay?"

"Nikki, get the hell out of here. Dean will be home soon and I have to pick Nard up from daycare." Rhonda protested as she took the towel Nikki was holding and wrapped it around her.

"Baby you don't have to cover up. Mama has seen it all before." Nikki bellowed. "And why did you hire a damn Nanny if you were going to have to pick him from daycare? Let Karen do that. Anyway, I plan to be gone in an hour. If it gets too good to us, Karen can take the kids to eat pizza or something."

She pulled Rhonda into a strong embrace. "I've been thinking about you and my moist cookie. I can't get you off my mind. I know you've missed me too, haven't you? Tell me that you miss me and you want me to taste that cookie." She kissed Rhonda on the face.

Rhonda released herself from Nikki's grip. "Where is Karen?" She asked.

"Don't worry. She's around." Nikki answered. "Ka-ren!" She yelled.

Within minutes Karen appeared in the doorway. She didn't say anything while she observed the scene in front of her. Rhonda held on to the towel, which was around her waist exposing her breast fully.

Nikki walked to Karen. We are about to have some private time. In about an hour, you will need to pick Nard up from daycare. Until then, why don't you just have a seat on that make-up bench? Mama is going to help Rhonda dry off."

Rhonda watched as Karen walked quietly to the bench. "No Nikki!" She exclaimed. "Stop! You need to leave. Bernard will be-

"Be what?" Nikki stopped her. "Be calling soon? I know about his lil ole EC conference. He's not going to interrupt this. I have plans for my cookie."

Rhonda wondered how Nikki knew about the conference. Had she been keeping up with Bernard's schedule or had Karen told her? Was Karen some sort of damn spy? She didn't know what to think. "No Nikki, I don't think-"

Before she could finish her sentence, Nikki grabbed her face under her chin and squeezed it. "Did...I ...ask...you...what...the ...fuck you...damnit...think?" She looked Rhonda in the eyes. "DID I?" She shouted. "Are you trying to make Mama mad?"

"No." Rhonda whispered. She slowly walked to the bed and let the towel drop to the floor.

"Do you want Karen to watch or not?" Nikki asked with a slight smile.

"Huh?" Rhonda responded.

"Never mind." Nikki said. "Mama is running this shit. Lay your ass on the bed."

Rhonda climbed to the middle of the bed and laid back. She bent her knees and spread her legs while Nikki undressed. Karen remained silent as she watched Nikki lick her tongue around her lips.

Nikki looked at Karen. "What are you looking at? Get your ass over there and help her get ready for Mama."

Karen stood. "What do you want me to do Nikki?" She asked.

"Don't play stupid bitch. You know what to do. And if you don't I will give you a minute to figure the shit out." She shouted.

Without undressing, Karen climbed on the bed and in between Rhonda's legs. She licked her clit slowly at first and gradually with more momentum. She stuck her finger in and out of Rhonda's opening as Rhonda moaned and rotated her body.

"Yes! Oh that feels good." Rhonda said loudly.

In an instant, Nikki grabbed Karen by the back of her shirt and pulled her off Rhonda. "That's enough. Let me do this. You too damn greedy. I want to finish eating the rest of this cookie. Isn't that what you want Rhonda? Don't you want mama to make you feel good?" She asked.

Rhonda was quiet. She had enjoyed Karen. The Latino beauty was smooth and tender as she made love to her. Nikki didn't have to stop her. Karen was handling her business. She wanted so badly for Karen to take her there but she knew better than to relate those feelings to Nikki.

"Where is your strap-on?" Nikki asked. "I'm goanna fuck you before I eat my cookie.

"I don't have it any more." Rhonda answered.

Nikki looked angry as she stood over Rhonda. "Did I fuckin tell you to get rid of it? Why the hell did you throw it away? Has that stupid ass husband of yours been fucking you? Huh?" She screamed. "Has he?"

When Rhonda didn't answer soon enough, Nikki slapped her pussy hard with an open hand. "Has that limp dick bastard been messing with my damn cookie?"

"Ouch Nikki. You're hurting me." Rhonda answered as she attempted to sit up.

Nikki knocked her back down on the bed while Karen watched. She wanted to intervene but Karen felt like to do so would be one of the biggest mistakes of her life. If she so much as mumbled a word, she feared that Nikki's rage would be redirected towards her. She felt helpless as she watched Nikki ram two fingers into Rhonda. She observed how fast and aggressively Nikki went in and out of her. Rhonda grimaced as she was being abused until Karen could no longer take it.

"Stop Nikki! What the hell are you doing? You are hurting her!" Karen yelled.

Nikki stopped and looked at Rhonda. "I'm sorry Babe. I didn't mean to hurt my cookie. Will you forgive me? I just blanked there for a minute." She kissed Rhonda on the cheek. "Am I forgiven? I'm so sorry that you make Mama do these things. I'm trying my best to keep things fresh but sometimes I really do think you are trying to spoil it."

There was no response from Rhonda. She just lay there wondering how long she was going to have to put up with Nikki being there. She wanted to be free of that bitch.

"Come on Karen and let me walk you out so you can get that kid from daycare." Nikki said. "And please make sure you are back in time to get that girl off the bus before she starts ringing the doorbell. Rhonda and I have some unfinished business."

Karen stood there; she didn't know the kids well enough to be keeping them occupied while Nikki was occupying their mom. "Come the hell on? What are you waiting for?" She asked Karen in a raised voice before turning to Rhonda. "Don't you move a muscle Boo. Mama will be right back."

Rhonda lay there not knowing what to expect as Karen walked out the door with Nikki trailing behind.

Once they were out of the room, Nikki shoved Karen into the banister. With her hands around Karen's throat she applied pressure while her victim gasped for air. "I ought to throw your damn ass over." She whispered in Karen's ear. "Don't ever make that mistake again. First you tried to eat all of my damn cookie when you knew full well that I only meant for you to have a taste. Then you have the damn nerve to interfere when I am handling my business." She released Karen, who hung over the banister taking in short breaths. "Try that shit again and I'll kill your Latino ass. Now get the fuck out of here while I take care of my cookie."

Karen hurried down the steps while Nikki walked back into the bedroom. "Are you all right? Mama didn't mean to hurt you. I don't like being rough with you. I'm going to make it up to you." She kissed Rhonda on the lip. "All I want is to make you feel good. Please let Mama love you." She seemed to be almost begging.

Rhonda relaxed and let Nikki take care of her. She couldn't deny that Nikki knew what to do to make her feel good. Even though Karen was good, she was nothing compared to Nikki who was also very attentive and caressing. Rhonda was in another zone and on the edge of a climax when Nikki stopped.

"Don't stop. Why did you stop?"

"I wanted to ask you something."

"What Nikki?"

"Did you like it when Karen ate my cookie?" She questioned.

Oh Shit! Here we go with the fuckin drama. "Nah! She wasn't all that." Rhonda answered.

"I love you Rhonda." Nikki said as she moved to the head of the bed to kiss Rhonda. She cuffed Rhonda's left breast and sucked it.

Although she wanted to relax, Rhonda had become tense. From previous experiences, she had no idea what to think after Nikki had asked that question concerning Karen. As Nikki moved to the other breast Rhonda began to feel more comfortable. Then she felt pressure being applied to her nipple as Nikki squeezed it and licked her nipple.

"Um…wonder how you would feel if I just bit this nipple off. Would that feel good to you or would it hurt."

"Please don't." Rhonda pleaded while Nikki squeezed harder. "Please Nikki. That will hurt."

"Well in that case you will feel like I felt when you were moaning and groaning while Karen was eating my damn cookie. Then you want to insult my fuckin intelligence by telling me that she wasn't all that. WHAT THE FUCK WAS YOU MOANING FOR?" She screamed.

"I don't know." Rhonda mumbled. "I just did but you are all I want. You make me feel good. It is all about you Mama."

Nikki let go of Rhonda's breast nipple. She kissed her forehead. "Mama is so sorry Baby. I don't know what is wrong with me lately. I just get so jealous at times. I know that nobody makes you feel like I do. Please don't be mad at me. Let's forget about Karen. Right now it is all about us. The two of us. Nobody else matters. I love you. Do you love me?"

"Yes." Rhonda answered.

"Tell me you love me." Nikki told her.

"I love you."

"Tell me you won't spoil it."

"I won't spoil it."

"Then lay your ass back and let Mama feast." Nikki slid down in the bed quietly whispering, "Until death does us apart."

Chapter 37

Anthony glanced at his watch. He was fifteen minutes early for his appointment with the lawyer Erik had provided for him. He was not as nervous as he had been. Redd had visited him earlier and was still down with the plan. He had agreed to come forward and claim the drugs as his own. In return Anthony would look out for his family and make sure they were looked after and taken care of. He would have Redd's back and when Redd had finished doing his bid, he would come out to a nice house and car which would be paid for, as well as money to start over with.

"Okay Mr. Woodruff." The receptionist stated. "Mr. Chambers will see you now. You can go right in."

Anthony replaced the *Jet* magazine on the table. Until the receptionist called him, he had been flipping through the pages, although he had obtained his GED he still didn't read too well.

Mr. Chambers sat in a high wing back leather chair and ruffled through some papers on his desk. His glasses rested on his nose and his hair was bald on top leaving only hair on the back and side of his head. "Have a seat." He told Anthony.

Once seated, Chambers gave him a copy of some papers to look at.

"Young man, you've dug quite a hole for yourself but I'm going to try to help you climb out of it. I'm going to make a motion to suppress any and all evidence, including specifically alleged crack cocaine and firearms, seized during a search of your premises."

"Can ya really do dat?" Anthony asked.

"Well I'm going to try my damnest. I contend that the search violated your Fourth Amendment right against unreasonable search and seizure, as well as your right under 18 U.S.C.3109 and Federal Rule of Criminal Procedure 41(d).

Anthony smiled even though he didn't understand exactly what Chambers was saying. "Splain dat please." He told Mr. Chambers. "Wat up?"

"The officers did not knock on your door or otherwise announce their presence. Rather they immediately forced their way into the house where they found you and your girlfriend Brandi in the bedroom." He continued. "The Fourth Amendment prohibits unreasonable search and seizures."

Anthony smiled. He felt at ease knowing that the police might not be able to use the evidence against him. He might be able to avoid caring for Redd's family. Hopefully, with no evidence, his case would be thrown out of court.

"Don't misunderstand me Mr. Woodruff. Because we file a motion to suppress doesn't mean we will be granted that motion. Title 18, United States Code, Section 3109 provides that an officer may open an outer or inner door or window of a house to execute a search warrant if after notice of his authority and purpose he is refused admittance or when necessary to liberate himself or a person aiding him in the execution of a warrant."

"So do dat mean dey had da rite ta break da door in?" Anthony asked.

"No!" Mr. Chambers answered. "In your case, the officers gave no notice of their authority and purpose, nor were they refused admittance to the house by you. They simply forced their way into the house."

"Ah! Now I see wat ya sayin." Anthony replied.

"What about Brandi? How does she stand on all of this? Are the two of you still in a relationship?"

"Nah. Not really. We still friends but I don moved on wit sumbody else." He answered.

"So, is she going to be a problem? You know they will try to get to her and have her turn States evidence for a deal. You do know that don't you?"

"Yeah, I know but she cool."

When Anthony finished talking with Mr. Chambers, the two shook hands. "Don't worry Mr. Woodruff. Without any unforeseen problems, I think we will be just fine."

A jubilant Anthony left Mr. Chambers office full of hope and confident that he would remain a free man. He felt as if the weight of the world had been lifted off his shoulders. When he got into his car, he retrieved his cell phone from the glove compartment. He had placed it in there before going into the Attorney's office to keep from being distracted. When Anthony looked at the phone he had twelve missed calls and four voice messages. He pressed the number one key and *talk* to listen to his voice messages. All four of them said the same thing. "Anthony, this is Brandi. Give me a call. It's important."

Without hesitation, he hit Brandi up on speed dial. Her phone rolled right over to voicemail. Anthony ended the call without leaving a message. He wondered what was so urgent. *Dat dam muthafuckin Detective Todd Foster betta not be houndin hur. I know dat shit. He betta not be fuckin wit hur and tyrna git hur ta tell him sum shit bout me. She sounded scared.* He didn't know what to think. He had twelve missed calls from Brandi and now she was not available. She wasn't working because the V.A. Medical Center had placed her on leave pending the outcome of the trial. Whatever she was calling about had to be urgent. He turned the key in the ignition and headed for Brandi's house. There was no guarantee that she would be there but she had to come home sooner or later.

Chapter 38

Karen was surprised to see Lance down the hall talking with Mrs. Covington. He was scheduled to be off and had not volunteered to do any overtime since the night he helped Nikki escape. The conversation looked intense from where she was standing. She wondered what the two were talking about.

Before she finished her rounds, Karen heard Lance calling her name. She turned and observed him standing in front of the break room. When she turned and walked in his direction, he entered the break room.

Karen figured no one was in there and Lance had some kind of crazy ass message to give her from Nikki but why would his stupid ass want to talk about it at work instead of waiting to get away from Brooksville? She didn't feel comfortable talking there. When she entered the break room, it was empty, as she had suspected.

"What's up Lance? What are you doing up in here on your day off?" She asked him.

"I need the money." He answered. "My funds are low. Also I need to talk to you." He looked around the empty room and towards the door. Then he brought his voice down to a whisper. "We are going to have to do something about Nikki."

"Well if you would have listened to me in the first place we would all be better off. I told you it was a bad fuckin idea to break her the hell out of here in the first place. But nah! Your ass was so in love." She whispered back.

"Thanks for reminding me but this is not the time for that *I told you so* shit." He responded. "I've been stealing meds from other people to give Nikki and she is not taking them. She has become more agitated. If we don't do something, this shit is going to blow up in our faces." He exclaimed.

"What the hell do you want me to do Lance. This is your mess; not mine. You are the one who created this hell. That lunatic almost threw me over a balcony the other day." Karen grabbed her chest as she recalled the frightening scenario with Nikki. She sat in a chair close to the door so she could hear if anyone walked up. They could both lose their jobs behind Nikki.

"Lance, let's do this." Karen suggested. "Let's table this conversation until we get off from work. I need to finish my rounds and I have already been in the break room for too long."

"Okay! But right after work, we can meet at the coffee shop. We need to take care of this Karen." He told her and stood.

The break room door swung open and Mrs. Covington walked in. "There you are young man. I was wondering where you had gotten to. Don't forget. I'm going to have you some peach cobbler tomorrow. I'll fix you a mighty heap. Now, if you stop by the store and get you some ice cream and heat that cobbler in the microwave and let that ice cream melt over it, you will have you some sho-nuff good eatin Son." She rubbed her stomach.

Karen giggled and nodded in agreement. "How are your grandchildren, Mrs. Covington?"

"Honey they are doing just fine. My older daughter and her husband have them. I'm so thankful they moved back in town. That baby girl of mine just doesn't seem to want to clean herself up. She's not a bad person. She just got out there with the wrong people and got on that stuff. I'm praying for her. I know that God is able."

"Yes He is." Karen responded. "Keep praying for her and I will do the same."

Lance strolled towards the door. "If you ladies will excuse me, I'm on the clock for another three and a half hours so I better get back to work."

"Me too." Karen said as she followed Lance. "It was nice talking to you. Try not to worry so much about your daughter. She'll get it together."

Mrs. Covington fidgeted with her hands. "I'm not worried so much about my daughter as I am this Nicole Harris stuff. You know…I think those detectives believe I had something to do with that. I done worked all these years and now this. I wouldn't mess up my name by doing something so stupid. Lawd, have mercy."

Lance and Karen glanced at each other. "Don't you worry about that." Lance stated. "I'm sure they are going to catch her soon."

"I doubt it honey. She's been out there a long time. I am sure that she is probably long gone by now." Mrs. Covington shook her head. "Long gone."

"Well let's hope not." Karen looked away. "Come on. Let's get back to work."

"You two hurry on along. I'm just goanna sat here a minute longer."

When the two were out of earshot, Lance spoke barely above a whisper. "Don't play around after work. I'll be waiting for you. We need to go ahead and take care of this soon."

"I'll be there." Karen told him. "I sure do hope you have a plan because I don't have one." She walked away to make her rounds.

****

When Karen pulled into the parking lot of the coffee shop, she spotted Lance's car. There were only a few people in the coffee shop and as soon as she walked in she observed Lance on the corner drinking coffee and eating what looked like a cheese Danish. After she paraded over to where he was, she sat across from him in the booth.

"Okay. I'm here Lance." Karen seemed anxious. "What is the brilliant plan?"

"Wait a minute. Slow down." He put his hands up as if he were a police officer halting traffic.

"Lance, I can't be here all day with this. I have to go on my other job. I know that bitch is crazy as hell but you are the one who unleashed her ass on the world. I told you that shit was a bad idea. But nah! You went ahead and did it anyway. Plus, you dragged me into the shit." She slightly raised her voice at Lance who took another sip of his coffee.

The waitress approached the table with the coffee pot and poured Lance a refill. "May I take your order ma'am?"

"Sure. I'll have a latte." Karen answered.

"Anything to eat?"

"No thank you. I'm good."

They watched while the waitress strolled away. "Karen, we have to find a way to turn Nikki in or set her up to be caught. We have to do it in a way that we won't be implicated. She is out of control and if we don't do something soon, she is still going to go down but the difference is that she will drag us down with her. Right now, she is obsessed with Rhonda. That's something we can use to our advantage. We just have to get Rhonda on board."

"Lance, I don't know. I'm not sure what the connection is there. I'm not sure if Nikki has something on Rhonda or if she is just scared of the lunatic or what."

"Well since you work there part-time, can't you find out? You will need to do it soon."

Karen's mind reflected back to the ordeal in Rhonda's bedroom. She didn't know what to think. She and Lance had basically let Nikki continue to manipulate them out of fear for job security. But Rhonda didn't seem to have anything to fear.

"I need to be getting out of here soon. I'll see what I can find out but what do you want her to do? How do you think Rhonda can help us?" Karen was curious.

"My plan is not complicated. We just need Rhonda to set Nikki up to meet her. We will call with an anonymous tip and Nikki will be captured. You and I won't even be involved. Nikki won't turn us in if it happens like that because she will feel like she can use us later. You know how Nikki is. It'll work." He told her.

"I don't know." Karen put a five-dollar bill on the table and stood. "It sounds kind of shaky to me. Suppose Nikki doesn't show up? Suppose she finds out we are involved in setting her up? Than what?"

"Stop with all the damn suppose shit. Suppose they don't catch her ass and she continues to make us her damn puppets on a string? Suppose that!" He snapped.

"Never mind Lance. We'll talk more about it later. Gotta go. I'll try to see what I can find out from Rhonda." She scurried out the door.

Chapter 39

When Brandi got home, Anthony was in the lawn chair waiting for her arrival. He had been at her house for about forty-five minutes waiting on her. Whatever she was calling for had to be urgent. The last time he had seen her, she stated that she didn't want to be his friend, right before putting him out of her house.

"Hey Brandi. Wat's goin on?" He asked. "I got ya messages. Wat's wromg? Ya wudn't be callin lik dat unless sumthin happen. Did dat muthafucka Foster mess wit ya? Talk ta me."

"Come on in Anthony." She told him while she quickly opened the door and hurried inside. "Have a seat. Want something to drink?"

"Nah Brandi. Wat up?"

"You already know there is nothing between us Anthony. We are not even friends. In fact, I despise the hell out of you for the way you deceived me. That was uncalled for. You didn't have to do me like that and I will never forgive your ass."

Is dis wat da fuck her dam ass wuz callin lik a fool fer? I don hurd dat shit befor.

Brandi continued. I found out something today that I think you need to know about. It's very important and could make a difference in whether or not you remain free."

So dat muthafuckin Foster DID git to hur. "Wat is it Brandi? Why ya always hafta beat round da damn bush? Wat da I need ta no?" He asked impatiently.

"Didn't I tell you not to trust Redd? I told you that your boy was a snake. Did you know he has talked to the detectives?" She asked.

"Ah shit. Gurl, ya don no wat ya talkin bout. Ya got it all wron. Dey musta question him lik dey did me. Dat's my dawg. He ain't gon tell nunthin ta hurt me. I thot ya had sum shit. Dat ain't nunthin." He stood to leave. "Tanks anyway gurl. Ya had a brotha scared shitless."

"Fool, Redd has given them information on you. He is going to testify against you. They didn't ask him to come in. He walked in on his own. He's giving them enough to put your black ass away. That's what your damn dawg has done for you. I tried to tell you he wasn't shit but you had your head so far up Erik's ass that your ears were stopped up." She continued. "My girlfriend that works in the D.A.'s office gave me the scoop."

"Datz a fuckin lie. She musta got Redd mixed up wit sumbody else. I no Redd and I'm telling ya he wudn't do no shit lik dat." Anthony opened his cell phone and dialed Redd's number. It went to voice mail. He tried again. "I can't git him on da fone but I'm tellin ya dat shit ain't rite."

"How damn stupid can you be man? He's giving them the dirt on you to save his own ass."

"Datz how I no ya don no wat da hell ya talking bout. He ain't got ta save hisself. Save hisself fer wat? Dey ain't got nunthin on him." Anthony continued to walk towards the door until Brandi made an outburst.

"They caught his ass with crack cocaine during a traffic stop so I would think they have something on his ass. The dogs conveyed on his jeep and he had a large amount of cocaine and cash. I heard that he was charged with drug trafficking."

Anthony faced Brandi, looking her straight in the eyes. "How ya no dis? Nah! Datz a lie. He wuda called me ta go his bail. Redd my dawg. He ain't gon let dem bitches talk him inta nunthin."

"If you say so." Brandi responded. "I don't put anything past him. He is trying to save his own ass. If he has to bury you in the process then that is exactly what he'll do."

"He my damn rite hand man. Dis shit cant be happenin." Anthony dialed Redd's number again. "FUCK!" He screamed as the call rolled over to voicemail again. "I gotta go. Tanks Brandi." He dashed out leaving the door open behind him.

Chapter 40

"Last day of the conference. Thank goodness." Bernard told his co-workers as they sat at the bar having drinks. "It's been a long one. I think I am going to turn in."

"What?" One of the guys replied. "Do you mean that you are turning in after only two drinks?"

"This has to be a first." Another added.

"Whatever." Bernard told the guys as he slid his chair back. "I'll see you all on the plane in the morning."

As soon as Bernard stepped onto the elevator to go to his room, he wondered about Rhonda. *Um...I wonder what kind of mood she will be in when I get home. Maybe absence does make the heart grow fonder. I miss her but lately it seems as if we are on separate pages. With Nard being autistic, he puts even more of a strain on our relationship.*

Bernard unlocked the door to his room. He kicked off his shoes and fell back on the bed fully dressed. When he thought he heard a noise, he sat up in bed and looked around the room but didn't see anyone. He got out of bed and looked in the bathroom. After pulling back the shower curtains and feeling like a paranoid fool, he decided it was his imagination. *I can't put this one on having too many drinks because I only had two.*

Bernard undressed and relaxed on top of the covers. He heard another noise. *Now I know good and damn well that I am not crazy.*

Suddenly the closet door opened and Nikki paraded out in full view, naked as hell. Without making any attempt to get up, Bernard fixated on Nikki as she slowly strolled towards the bed.

"How the hell did you get in here Nikki?" He questioned.

"That's not important." She answered. "What's important is that I brought this good pussy to you. But if you don't want it, I'll just take my juicy wet pussy and walk right on up out of here."

He slowly stroked his magic stick with his hand. "Why the hell do you keep fucking with me Nikki?"

She ignored him and put one foot on the bed. With two fingers she spread the lips of her pussy. After licking one finger she inserted it into her opening. "Um…I need to cum." She whispered to Bernard in a sexy seductive voice.

Bernard stroked his magic stick harder as he licked his lips. "Get over here and let me fuck you Nikki. Come on and get what you came for." He stood and helped Nikki to the center of the bed. After putting his arms under her legs, he slid her to the edge of the bed.

"You know I want this pussy don't you?" He slid his magic stick into her wetness. "Damn, this pussy is hot. It feels good to Daddy. Throw that pussy."

He went in and out of Nikki while she lay on her back massaging her breast. "Is this pussy still good to you?" She asked.

"You know it is." He answered. "I always want to fuck you Nikki. Ump! Ah damn. Baby…this… pussy… feels so good to me."

"Is this still my dick?" She asked.

"Yeah bay…bee." He spoke in a soft voice. "Yeah."

"Let me on top. I want to ride that dick."

He let her legs down. When she got up, he stretched out on his back and his magic stick stood at attention. Nikki couldn't resist putting it in her mouth before climbing on top of him. She rubbed the hairs on his chest while she galloped on his stiffness.

"Ah Nikki." He moaned. "Oh damn!"

"Is this the best pussy you've ever had?" She asked.

Bernard held on to her thighs. It felt good having his dick in her. "Oh Baby. Ride this horse." He began to speak louder.

"I asked you if this was the best damn pussy you ever had. Tell me Boo. Tell me cause I am ready to cum for you."

"Yeah Nikki. Hell yeah. This ...is...the ...best...augh...pus...sy! Ahh! I'm cumming!"

He squeezed her as his body went into shimmers.. "Augh...day...am!"

Nikki climbed down from him. "That was good. I love the feeling of your juices traveling through my body."

"Shit!" Bernard seemed to snap back into reality. "Nikki this shit has to stop. We can't keep doing this. Leave me and my family the hell alone."

"Leave you alone? Is that what you said muthafucka? I'm not bothering you. I brought the pussy to you but I didn't put a gun to your damn head did I? Hell no. You wanted me. You are like any other damn man. You see pussy and you want to put your damn dick in it. How the fuck do you sound talking about leave your ass alone?"

Bernard was speechless. He knew that Nikki was right. She had not forced him to have sex with her. He wanted it. He wanted to feel himself inside of her. He only prayed that Rhonda would never find out. Nikki meant nothing to him. It was only sex. Nothing more. That damn Nikki just had a way of seducing his mind. Rhonda was the woman he loved. *Damn! I have to exhibit better control. I cannot get tied up with Nikki again.*

He heard the water running and knew Nikki was taking a shower. He remembered the many nights he and Nikki had showered together. They would lather each other before going for another round in the shower. While he thought about Nikki getting lathered in the shower, his magic stick began to grow. Bernard lightly patted it with an open hand. *Nah boy. Calm your ass down, Easy does it. Just stay down there.* Since Bernard's magic stick didn't want to be obedient he began to rub it. *What the hell? This will be the last time.* He got out of bed with his magic stick in his hand and headed for the shower.

Chapter 41

Karen arrived at Rhonda's house two hours early. "I know that I am early but I pulled a double and didn't want to oversleep."

"That's fine. You're welcome to take a nap. It'll be a minute before you have the kids. Bernard missed his plane and had to catch a later flight so he'll be late. I don't mind. Make yourself comfortable in one of the guest rooms." Rhonda suggested.

"I don't want to fall asleep but I think I will lay across the bed and rest?" She replied.

Karen chose the guest room with the black and silver interior. The room was beautiful She hoped to one day be able to afford a nice house. *I won't need a house if Lance and I don't get rid of Nikki. Why will I need a house when they have one uptown already furnished off for me? What I really need to do is find out what was up with Rhonda and Nikki. I wonder if Rhonda would be willing to help set Nikki up.*

"Are you all right in here?" Rhonda asked as she stuck her head in the door.

"I'm fine. Come on in. I'd like to ask you something."

Rhonda entered the bedroom and took a seat on the black ottoman. "I am all ears. What's up?" She asked.

"I really don't know how to ask you this so I will come right on out and ask. What is the deal with Nikki and you? How did you get involved with her? You have a nice ass husband. Are you bi-sexual?"

"Hold up." Rhonda looked at her. "When you said you'd like to ask me something, I didn't realize it would be an interrogation about my personal life." She responded. "I could ask you the same question. I could ask you how you let yourself get involved in helping her escape. Don't you know they could put your ass under the jail for that?"

"Look Rhonda. I'm sorry. I never should have pried into your personal life. It's none of my business. As for Nikki and me, I think I told you before that I was vulnerable. I had just ended a relationship and I was not thinking. Nikki took advantage of my vulnerability. She preyed on me and by the time I realized what had gone down, it was too late. I either had to help her or let her ruin my life and reputation. I chose to help her. Although I must admit that now I am having second thoughts."

Rhonda listened to everything Karen said without interrupting. After she had finished speaking, Rhonda spoke. "I am not bi-sexual. My husband and I were having some problems. Nikki was aware of this and like with your situation, she took advantage." Rhonda decided not to mention the threesome. She didn't see the need in telling all of her business. "I later found out the bitch had been sleeping with my husband. The affair she and Bernard had resulted in us having these children. I don't blame them though. It is not their fault."

"Damn!' Karen exclaimed. "That a bitter pill to swallow, if you don't mind me saying. Don't you ever think about getting revenge on her? My goodness, the woman had an affair with your husband."

"I don't know Karen. I never thought about revenge. I know that I have done some wrong things myself and I don't claim to be a Christian. But I do remember growing up that my parents and grandparents always said that vengeance belongs to the Lord." Her mind drifted back to the way Bernard seemed to enjoy having his magic stick in Nikki and the way he cried out like someone had just poured hot grits on him. "Besides, it takes two. Nikki was not solely the blame. My husband played a role in it also." She looked away.

Both women were quiet for a moment until Karen rolled over on the bed and rested her elbows on the bed with her chin in her hands. "Rhonda, what's going to happen when they finally catch Nikki?" She asked. "What's going to happen to all of us who knew where she was and didn't turn her in? She is a felon and they consider her dangerous."

"THEY! They consider her dangerous? And you don't?" She questioned Karen. "How many times has she snapped and laid hands on you?"

Karen was quiet. She knew Rhonda was telling the truth.

"How many Karen?' she asked again. "Has she ever choked you? Kicked you? Drugged you? Well I've been through it all and then some. There is no doubt in my mind that Nikki is dangerous. She killed her cousin in a failed attempt to kill one of my friends. I don't trust her and I don't put anything past her." Rhonda stood.

"If that's how you truly feel then help Lance and me. We are trying to get her locked back up where she belongs. She needs to be in somebody's maximum-security prison. Brooksville and other mental hospitals are not equipped to deal with a woman like Nikki. She is too cunning and manipulative. She gives the impression that she is sane but inwardly that bitch has some deep rooted problems." Karen sat up in the bed. "She doesn't need to be out here free styling like she is."

"I agree that she needs some help and meds. There is no doubt about that but what do you and Lance have in mind? I hope you both know that it has to be one-hundred percent guaranteed to work; because if it doesn't, Nikki will not think twice about killing you."

"We know that." Karen remarked. "That's where you come in at. We are going to need your help. Nikki is obsessed with you. We can't do this without you Rhonda. Will you please help us?" She pleaded.

In a raised voice with one finger pointed in Karen's face, Rhonda cried, "Hell to the capital N, capital O, capital NO!"

Karen felt as if she had made a mistake by asking Rhonda to help her and Lance. They were on their own It would be so much better if they could depend on Rhonda because Nikki seemed to eat, sleep, and breathe Rhonda. Oh well…She and Lance would have to come up with a plan B.

Chapter 42

Anthony stepped out onto the church steps. He had found himself in the familiar place his grandmother had always brought him as a child. The elderly women gave him hugs and kisses. The men shook his hand.

"How are you Brother Woodruff? It's good to have you back in the fold." One of the older men said to Anthony as he extended his hand.

"Amen!" One of the women said. "I know that your grandmother is dancing around Heaven. I bet she doing the happy jig on them golden streets."

"Yes Ma'am." Anthony responded. "I no she lookin down on me. I miss hur a lot. Well, I gotta git goin. I gotta lot of stuff I need ta do. Enjoyed da service."

Anthony was surprised to see so many people present. He didn't think large crowds turned out like that for Wednesday night Bible Study. After speaking to a few more people he got in his car and headed to the Waffle House to grab a bite to eat before turning in. When he entered the Waffle House he saw that, it too was crowded. Anthony took a seat at the counter. Before he glanced at the menu, he heard someone call his name.

"Hey Anthony! Over here."

He turned to see his ole pal Duke seated in a booth at the back of the restaurant. Duke waved his hand for Anthony to join him.

Hey man. I dint see ya car out der wen I pulled up. I dint know watz up. Is everythin gud?"

"Yeah. Everything is straight." Duke answered. "I've just been chillin and taking it easy."

The waitress approached the table. "What can I get you gentlemen to drink?"

"Coke." Anthony answered.

"Make that two." Duke said.

"Do you want to order now or do you need a few more minutes." She asked.

"We're ready." Duke told the waitress. "Let me have the pork chop plate. Hash browns, smothered, covered and scattered."

"And I guess I will hav da t-bone plate wit a bowl of grits. Make da steak well done cuz I don wanna see blood wen I eat."

As soon as the waitress left the table, Anthony directed this attention to Duke. "How did thins go man?"

"I told you everything is good. I don't play around. You should know that."

"Yeah man. I no ya don but I been stress like a mutha. Dis court shit got my nerves on edge. I'm not goin back in dat damn hellhole." Anthony stuck his hand in his inside jacket pocket. He pulled out the long envelope and slid it across the table. Duke opened the envelope and looked inside.

"It's all der man." Anthony said.

"Thanks." Duke said. "I hope they hurry with the food. I'm starving."

Anthony's phone rang. He looked at the number and wondered why Brandi was calling. She had made it clear that there could be no friendship between them. Was it possible that she was having trouble turning her feelings off? He answered the telephone.

"Yeah Brandi. Wat up? Oh no! Wen? How bad is it? Nah, I hant hurd nunthin bout dat. I been in Bible Study. Ok. Ima hafta go check on his famlee. Thans fer keepin me in da loop." He ended the call.

"That conversation didn't sound so good. Is everything all right?" Duke asked just as the waitress sat their food on the table.

"Ya rite Duke. Dat news wuz not gud atall." Anthony shook his head. "My dawg got shot tanite while I wuz in church. Dey don hav no idea who dun it. I feel bad bout dat shit. I shuda had my ass der with him and I mita been able ta do sumthin."

Duke had a smile on his face. "You could not have known Anthony. Don't beat yourself up over this. How is he? I'm sure that he will be all right."

"Man, my dawg is dead. Sumbody popped off fo shots in his head. Left him in a pool of his own blood. It wadnt no robbery. He had money on him and dey dint even take da money. Wonda wat cuda happen ta make sumbody kill him?"

"Oh well…too bad for your friend. He must have crossed the wrong one. Right? Let's not let it ruin a great meal." Duke took another bite of his food. "Um…um…umph! They make the best damn chops around."

"Eva time ya eat sumthin ya say itz da best round." Anthony laughed. "Man, I gotta split. Ima take care of da check and den Ima stop by Redd's house ta check on his peeps. Datz sum foul shit. Ta just lev my man out der in da streets lik dat, lik a dam animal or sumthin. I know dat ya headed back outta town and I won be seein ya. Thans fer everythin Duke." The two men shook hands and Anthony left.

Chapter 43

Bernard walked into the quiet house and dropped his things on the chair. He wondered where Rhonda and the kids were. At least with him having some time to himself, he could reflect on some things. *What the hell is it about Nikki that makes me come back for more? I love Rhonda and I know it would kill her if she found out I have been with Nikki again. Damn! I'm a man. Half the time Rhonda acts like she doesn't want me. I have needs.*

He went to the bar and fixed himself a drink before going into the den to grab the remote. As usual he flipped through a few channels before deciding to watch the news. After listening to a newscaster report on the capture of a teenager who had carjacked a woman and her son, he decided that nothing on the news is ever good.

Bernard had taken another sip of his drink when Nikki's picture flashed on the screen. A spokesperson from Brooksville was speaking. "It is our goal at Brooksville to provide true quality care. Our nurses and staff provide care twenty-four hours. Our psychiatrists provide evaluations, and maintain medication regimens. We also provide psychiatric treatment and counseling. We advocate for our patients and help them plan for discharges as well as learn how to regain control of their lives. We do not take the escape of Nicole Harris lightly. We are working very closely with authorities to resolve this matter and ensure that nothing of this nature happens again. Someone out there has seen something. We ask for the community to please come forth with any information, no matter how small. The longer Ms. Harris is without her medication, the more volatile the situation may become. If you have any information, please contact the number on the screen."

He was surprised to see they were still broadcasting Nikki on the news. There had to be more recent events to report on. Hadn't somebody got murdered or a house broken into or something. *If the authorities ever find out that I have been with Nikki since her escape, I will be ruined. No matter what; she is still the mother of my kids. I can't turn her in. I can't keep fucking her either. Whether she admits it or not, Nikki loves me. If she didn't, why would she keep coming back to me?*

The door opened and Dean ran in and jumped on Bernard's lap. "We had fun. Mama took us to Dairy Queen and I got my ice cream dipped in chocolate. Nard got ice cream all over his nose and face. He looked like a clown. It was so funny. You should have seen him Daddy."

"I bet that did look funny." Bernard told Dean as he bounced her on one knee. And guess what?"

"What?" She asked.

"We are really going to have some fun Saturday. We are going to the circus. You and your brother will be able to see all sorts of animals doing tricks. It will be exciting."

"Yippee!" Dean yelled. "I can't wait."

"What's all the commotion about?" Rhonda asked as she entered the room with Nard.

"Daddy said he's taking us to the circus Saturday." Dean answered excitedly. "We're going to have lots of fun. Nard is going to like that." She smiled.

"All righty Babe. You and Nard hang out in here for a while so I can talk to your daddy. Bernard, let me see you see in the bedroom."

"Sure Honey. I'll be right up. Let me freshen my drink." He answered.

He walked into the bedroom before Rhonda finished undressing. "What are you doing Rhonda? You know the kids are awake."

"It's ok." She responded. "They are downstairs. We are just going to get a quickie."

"Baby, it's not that I don't want to. That long ass conference and then the plane ride; I'm just exhausted. Let me get myself built back up."

"Back up from what?" She asked as she put her clothes back on. "Or do I already know? Have you been fucking somebody else?"

"Hell no Baby! Don't think any damn thing crazy like that. You know better."

"Actually I don't know any better. I didn't want your damn dick in me any way." Rhonda decided it was no use in calling the damn thing a magic stick any more because there was nothing magic about a stick that roamed where it didn't belong.

"What's wrong with you woman? I am just tired and you want to make a big damn deal out of it. Miss me with the bullshit. Damn!"

"Listen to me Bernard and listen well. I was only testing your lame ass. I was curious to see if you desired your wife as much as you desire your whore." Her voice was now elevated.

"What whore? I don't have a whore. What the hell are you talking about? Don't accuse me of shit when you don't have proof or know what the hell you are talking about. Just because I am tired doesn't mean I have been fucking around." He shouted. "I'm not going through this shit. All I said was wait until tonight so I could build myself up and right away you want to jump to some fuckin conclusions."

"It's fine Bernard because I don't want you any more so do you. Move the hell out and fuck whomever you want, whenever you want." She walked to the television, which was mounted, on the wall in the left corner of the room. After putting in a dvd she walked to the door. "I need to check on the kids. Fuck you Bernard." She exited the room.

Bernard sat on the bed until he heard his voice. *How the hell did you get in here Nikki?* He stood instantly gazing at the television screen as it pictured him stroking his magic stick and licking his lips. His heart beat faster as he listened to his own words *Get over here and let me fuck you. I'm going to give you what you came for.* He grabbed the bed while the movie played out with him telling Nikki how hot and good her pussy was and that the dick belonged to her. He was busted. Nikki had set him up.

Rhonda walked back into the room with tears in her eyes. "Did you enjoy the movie Bernard or are you going to tell me that wasn't you telling Nikki you always want to fuck her and that it was the best pussy you ever had?"

"Rhonda please." He begged. "She set me up. She was already in my room with camera set up when I got there. I didn't invite her ass. She did this. Can't you see? All she wants to do is break us up. Then she will be happy. Don't let her do this to us."

"She knew Bernard. That's why she had the camera set up. She knew you would fuck her. You don't give a damn about me. If you did, you would have told her to leave. But instead, you lay your ass there stroking your shit and licking your lips. I'm done."

"I do. I do love you. That's why I told her we couldn't keep doing it. I told her that. Didn't you hear me?" His eyes were begging for understanding.

"Yes Bernard. I did hear you tell her that. I believe you told her a few minutes before you decided to join her in the shower. How do you think I felt when this bitch flagged me down in front of the kids and said she had something important to show me? How the fuck do you think I felt when the kids were eating ice cream and the bitch pulled out a portable DVD player and I witnessed that shit and then had to keep my composure for the kids' sake? I told the bitch thanks and she left me looking like the biggest fool in the fuckin world? Get your shit and get the fuck out. NOW!" She screamed. "GO!"

"No Rhonda. I love you. Please don't make me leave. You and the kids are all that matter to me. I don't give a damn about Nikki. If you love me and I know that you do; we can find a way to work this out."

"Work this out? Motherfucka we worked it out when you brought your whore to me for gotdamn threesome knowing you had a baby by the bitch. We worked the shit out when you fucked her while I watched at gunpoint and your ass enjoyed it so fucking much that you nutted all up in her and got her pregnant again. There is no more working shit out except for you to work your ass out the fuckin door. Now Go!"

Bernard hung his head as he slowly walked out the door.

Chapter 44

Anthony felt confident as he walked into the courtroom with his attorney. He was dressed in a nice suit and tie as Mr. Chambers had suggested. He knew Brandi would not testify against him and the only other person who knew anything had been murdered. He felt sorry for Redd's family and made himself a mental note to take care of them.

After everyone stood for the judge, the proceedings began. Anthony wondered where Erik was. He had glanced around the courtroom upon entering and there was no sign of Erik. *Dis cud be gud or bad. Gud cuz he don thin he needa be here cuz he know everythin gon be fine. Or bad cuz he don wanna be here ta see me go down.*

He was deep in thought until he heard the Detective on the stand call Redd's name. He told how Richard "Redd" Lomax had been arrested. Redd had initiated contact with D.A. Foster and offered him information for a plea agreement. He had stated that he was the best friend and sidekick of Anthony Woodruff. He had stated that Anthony was the number one source for cocaine in the city.

"Objection!" Mr. Chambers said. "Not only is this hearsay but Mr. Lomax could not possibly have known who the number one source of cocaine was. Not unless he knew every single supplier."

"Objection Sustained. Jury will disregard," The Judge ordered.

Under cross-examination, the Detective told how Redd had stated he made approximately eight or nine trips to New York for cocaine. When the Detective stated that Anthony arranged all of the trips, his lawyer objected again.

Damn! Dat muthafucka ain't have no problem sellin a brotha out. He deserb ta be ten toez up. He continued to listen to the testimony.

Detective Foster spoke clear. "Richard usually purchased cocaine in half kilo and kilo quantities. Sometimes Woodruff would make a run in his truck and drop Richard off to get a rental car. Once Richard would rent a car and make a purchase, he would catch up with Woodruff later that night."

Anthony listened quietly. It was hard for him to contain himself knowing Redd had divulged so much information to save himself. When in fact, rather than save himself, it had cost him his life.

Dis shit lemme know ya cant trust no dam body wit shit. Dis muthafucka don tol bout da cars and da dam property I got. May dat son of a bitch rest in piss.

"Anthony, don't worry about any of that stuff. It is all hearsay. The Judge allowed it because they have a recorded statement from him but no expert or voice analysis has been brought into evidence to even verify that it was Richard on the tape. Richard is dead and no one can prove he said those things. I'll take care of that in closing remarks." Anthony let out a deep breath.

Wat da fuck? Wat da D.A. call Jessica ta da stan fer? Why da hell wud she testify fer dem. Hell…I treated hur ass decent. Now dat bitch up swarin ta tell da hole truf and nunthin but da truf.

"Would you state your name please?" The prosecution asked.

"Jessica Snider.'" She stated in a low voice.

"Keep your voice up so we can all hear you. It is a large courtroom. Ms. Snider do you know the defendant, Anthony Woodruff?" the D.A. asked Jessica.

"Yes."

"And when did you first meet him?"

"About six years ago. I dated him before he first got locked up. Then we started back dating after he was released." She answered.

"At some point did you and Mr. Woodruff become engaged?"

"Yes we did."

"Are you currently engaged?"

"No. I broke it off." She glanced briefly at Anthony.

"Now, just before he was arrested did you ever see any firearms at the defendant's residence?"

Jessica looked at Anthony again before answering. "Yes."

"Did you see Government's Exhibit #7, this SKS rifle inside his house?"

"Yes."

"And did you see Government's Exhibit #10, this AP-9 inside his residence?"

Again, her answer was yes.

"From conversations with Mr. Woodruff do you know who purchased the AP-9?" The D.A. questioned.

"Yes." She answered lowly. "His friend Redd."

"And would that be Richard Lomax?"

Jessica affirmed that it was Richard who had purchased the weapons. As the D.A. went on to question her. The courtroom was silent. She testified about how she never wanted to be involved in a drug operation. She stated that Anthony spent money without any regard to its value because he had so much. She said he had deceived her and was not the man she thought he was.

When Mr. Chambers cross-examined her, Jessica cried on the witness stand. "Did you prosper from the drug money?"

"Yes." She answered.

"Did Anthony purchase a car in your name and give it to you?"

"Yes he did.'

"You never witnessed Mr. Woodruff buying any drugs, did you?"

"No." She whispered.

"Speak up please. Keep your voice loud. As the D.A. stated, this is a large courtroom and it sort of swallows the sounds. Will you please repeat your answer?"

"No!" She said loudly.

"In fact, isn't it true that you were engaged to Mr. Woodruff and found a text on his telephone from someone else and that is what led to your breakup? And isn't it true that you told him you would make him pay if it were the last thing you did." The D.A. raised his voice.

"Yes!" Jessica stated clearly.

"No further questions your Honor."

The Judge spoke to the courtroom. "It is 12:30 p.m. Let's recess these proceedings and adjourn at 2:00 p.m."

Anthony smiled. He felt wonderful. Erik had indeed hired the right attorney. The courtroom was packed. He noticed Brandi there in a green dress and high heel shoes. She looked classy. He never understood how she could walk in those heels.

People scurried out of the courtroom. Brandi was walking in Anthony's direction when a shot rang out. Everybody scattered and ducked for cover. Brandi watched as Anthony clutched his chest before falling to the floor. She dashed to his side and kneeled next to him as blood seeped through his clothes.

"Get an ambulance." She screamed. "Help! Anthony, hang on. Help is on the way."

Two of the deputies quickly attended to Anthony. As the crowd thinned out, Brandi noticed the shooter. The woman stood there in a daze, holding the gun when authorities approached her. "Put the gun down Ma'am."

The woman handed the gun to the officer. Brandi pondered who the woman might be and wondered what would possess her to shoot Anthony.

Brandi looked at Anthony whose eyes were barely open. He murmured, "Brandi, I'm sorry I hurt ya. Tell Erik-" He closed his eyes just as the paramedics arrived.

"He would have gotten away with it. I couldn't let him ruin another life. I just couldn't. He ruined my daughter's life." Mrs. Covington cried as she was led away in handcuffs.

"You have the right to remain silent…"

Chapter 45

Rhonda looked around the room. Nothing was there that said Bernard would be back. His ties, his deodorant, his shaving supplies and clothing were all gone. This was great. Now, all she had to do was wait for Karen to get there. At first, she had been hesitant to go along with Karen and Lance's plan to set Nikki up but since she wanted to be the evil bitch that everyone portrayed her to be, she'd get exactly what the hell she deserved.

She went downstairs to fix herself a drink. *What makes the bitch think she can fuck my husband when she wants to and throw the shit up in my face? I can be a ferocious bitch when I wanna and Nikki is about to find out first hand. Let them lock her up and throw away the damn key.*

The doorbell chimed as Rhonda took another sip of her drink. She spoke into the intercom. "Yes?"

"It's me. Karen."

"Okay. One minute." She answered.

When Karen entered the house, Rhonda didn't waste any time. "I'm ready." She blurted out.

"Ready for what?" Karen inquired.

"Ready to help you and Lance set Nikki up. What's the plan?"

"Hold up. Calm down. What brought all of this on? Don't misunderstand this but I'm not sure we can trust you. When I first approached you with the idea, you were totally against it. So am I now supposed to believe that all of a sudden you had a change of heart?"

Rhonda took another sip of her drink. "Would you like me to fix you one?" She asked as she held her head up.

"Yes! I'll have one." Karen answered.

Rhonda poured Karen a drink and mixed it with a small amount of grapefruit juice. "I can understand you being cautious, and hesitant. I don't blame you. But I am ready to have Nikki out of our lives. She's a demon and she thinks her shit doesn't stink. It's time for her to be put away."

"I'm curious Rhonda. May I ask what changed your mind?"

"Is that relevant?"

"Well yes. I believe it is considering how fast you changed up."

"I told you before that Nikki and my husband had an affair which resulted in the kids. Do you remember?" She asked.

"Yeah. I remember you telling me that."

"Well this bold bitch has still been seeing my husband. I say bold because she videoed the shit and gave it to me. It was her way of letting me know that Bernard chose her pussy over mine and that she can have him any time she wants him."

"Damn!" Karen exclaimed. "What did he say about it?"

"What the hell could he say? He couldn't deny it when it played right in front of his ass. I put him out. Fuck him!" Karen could see the anger building up in Rhonda.

"I'm not trying to get in your business Rhonda but don't you think you have double standards? I mean like you have been with Nikki too. You did all of this behind your husband's back. He didn't do any worse to you then you did to him. Nikki could have just as easily set you up at my house and had a hidden camera. What if she had given Bernard a video of that day?"

Rhonda looked away. She knew that Karen was right. She had been caught in Nikki's web also. That still did not excuse Bernard. Karen didn't understand how hurtful it was. She had to come face to face with the fact that her husband desired another woman more than he desired her. It was painful to see how he could take a look at Nikki's naked body and his dick would come to life instantly.

"I realize that you are keeping it real with me and I appreciate it." She remarked. "But that still does not change the fact that Nikki needs to be stopped. It is time for her to get the help that she needs."

Karen glanced at her. "So are you ready to help Lance and me? Seriously?" She asked. "Once we start, there is no turning back. We will have to complete it no matter what."

"Yeah! I know. I'm ready. What's the plan? What do you and Lance have in mind and how can I help?"

"I'll call Lance so we can set things up. He can come over now if he is not busy. I think he has to work tonight."

"Okay. Let's do this." Rhonda said

"No turning back." Karen nodded in agreement.

Chapter 46

Brandi was frantic as she rode in the ambulance with Anthony to the hospital. When he went limp and his head fell to the side, she thought for sure that he had died in her arms. He looked so pale and there was so much blood. As the ambulance zoomed through the streets, slowing only at intersections with red lights or stop signs, Brandi prayed. *Oh Lord, please don't let him die. I know that he has done a lot of things that are against your will but he really doesn't know any better. He was just out there trying to make a quick dollar. Please forgive him. Even for his twisted sexual lifestyle. Lord, just don't let him die. I said some pretty bad things to him. Please give me a chance to make it right. I am not his Judge. Thank you Lord. Amen.*

When Brandi finished praying, Anthony batted his eyes. He tried to speak even though there was an oxygen mask covering his face. "Br-"

"Shhh! Don't try to speak." Brandi responded. "You're going to be all right. You've lost a lot of blood but you're going to be all right. I just know you are."

Anthony looked at her a moment before closing his eyes again.

Damn! Erik! I need to call Erik's ass. She opened her cell phone and dialed Erik's number. "Hello," she said when Erik answered his private number. "Yes, I figured you had patients today since I didn't see you in court. No! It's not over. The Judge recessed and some woman shot Anthony. No I'm not lying. I am in the ambulance with him now. They are transporting him to the hospital. It looks critical. What? I know you're not serious. You're a fuckin doctor. What the hell do you mean that you can't put your reputation on the line by coming to the hospital? He could be one of your patients. You are a damn joke. Goodbye!"

Brandi closed her cell phone and glanced at Anthony. His eyes remained closed but she saw tears strolling down the side of his face. She wondered if he had heard her conversation with Erik.

The ambulance pulled into the emergency entrance. A nurse directed Brandi to a waiting area while Anthony was swished down the hall. She couldn't believe the conversation she had just had with Erik. He didn't give a damn about Anthony. He was all for himself. If he cared the least little bit, he would have cancelled his patients for the day and rushed to the hospital. *And that's the shit he gave me up for. Damn! Was he too stupid to see that Erik was using him?*

Anthony had no blood pressure when he arrived and had slipped into a coma. He was bleeding internally. X-rays showed that the bullet had lodged millimeters from his heart. With blood entering his chest cavity the doctors knew his condition was serious. Erik acted as if he were not fazed by the whole ordeal.

Anthony was in surgery for two hours and still there was no sign of Erik. When he woke up the nurse gave him pain medication so he would be comfortable until he was weaned off the ventilator. He looked around the room past Brandi as if she were not there. She knew he was expecting to see Erik.

"He not here Anthony. He hasn't been here." Brandi hated to be so blunt but Anthony needed to face reality. And reality was that Erik had used him. Erik didn't give a damn about him. This man whom he loved so much and was willing to risk it all for didn't respect him enough to take five minutes to see if he was okay. She knew Anthony was hurt but he brought it on himself.

"Hey Brandi." He spoke slightly above a whisper.

"How do you feel?" She asked.

"Lik I've been shot." He tried to manage a smile. "Who shot me?"

"I don't know the full details." She answered. "What I do know is that it was an older woman. Her daughter is strung out on drugs and she had been raising her grandchildren until their aunt moved here. She somehow blames you. I don't know if her daughter knows you or if someone told her you were the supplier or what. From the details I received thus far, I know that her daughter overdosed and is on life support."

Anthony didn't respond. Instead he changed the subject. "Wat time is it? Is Erik off yet?"

"Did you hear me Anthony? Erik is not coming. He is not bringing his ass out here to see you. If he were coming, he would have been here by now. I called him hours ago. I told him that your condition was serious but he was worried about his reputation. He can't be seen here with you. How would it look to his colleagues?"

Anthony looked at her. "Ya wrung. He gon come. He must be waitin fer nite. Ya no how well nown he is." Anthony said the words but the look of concern on his face told a different story.

Brandi knew he wasn't as sure of Erik as he wanted her to believe. Maybe he was beginning to realize that Erik had used him all along. Maybe this was what it took for him to finally understand that he had only been a means to an end. He had made money for himself and had made much more for Erik. But in the end, when the chips were down, it was every man for himself.

Chapter 47

Rhonda wasn't nervous at all as she and Karen waited on Nikki to arrive. Lance had to make sure the timing was right. If he got the police there at the right time, it would look like Karen and Rhonda were victims and not like they had aided Nikki in her attempt to elude the authorities.

The doorbell rang and Karen spoke into the intercom. "May I help you?"

"Yes. You can help me. It's Nikki. Rhonda is expecting me."

"She told me. Hold on a minute. I'll let you in. You're a bit early. She's just getting out of the shower."

Nikki came in and looked around the room. "Don't you have work to do?" She asked Karen.

"Sure." Karen answered. "I was just taking a break while the clothes dry. I do a lil light duty work some days for a lil extra change. It helps to make up for the hours I miss with the kids."

"Hey! I thought I heard voices." Rhonda walked into the room with a towel wrapped around her. "I'm glad you came Nikki. I've been feeling on edge. Since I put Bernard out, it's been kind of lonely. At least he did make me feel wanted when he was here. And he satisfied my needs."

"Satisfied what needs?" Nikki snapped. "He didn't satisfy you half as much as I do. Nobody makes you feel like I do. You know it and I know it. Fuck you. He didn't want you. He wanted me. Haven't you figured that shit out by now?" She questioned Rhonda as Karen silently observed.

"Excuse me." Karen finally spoke. "I'll just go in the laundry room and check on those clothes." She turned to walk away Nikki grabbed her arm.

"Who told you that you could leave bitch?" She asked.

"I was just getting out of the way Nikki. I know that you didn't come here to see me. I was trying to give you and Rhonda some privacy."

"Privacy my ass!" She exclaimed. "You never worried about giving us privacy before. Get undressed and bring that juicy fruit to the bedroom."

Rhonda let the towel drop to the floor and stepped over it as she led the way to the bedroom.

Karen was nervous. She had no intention of participating. She planned to let Lance know when it was time to notify authorities. This had to go down today. They might not get another opportunity any time soon. She waited until she got to the bedroom to undress. Nikki stood in the middle of the room gazing at Rhonda.

"Is that Cookie ready for Mama?"

"Yes." Rhonda answered. "It's ready and I hope you are ready. I've missed you Nikki. Can this be our day? Does Karen have to be in on this? Why can't she wait until next time?"

Nikki glanced at Karen. "Come here." She demanded. "Bring that fruit to Mama."

Karen strolled her naked body over to Nikki and stood not knowing what to expect. Nikki could grab her and kiss her or Nikki could slap the taste out of her mouth. There was no telling. As she stood there,

Nikki suddenly grabbed her around the waist with one arm, and pulled her in closely. She felt Karen's breast before touching her fruit.

"That's what I like to feel. My fruit is juicy. Go ahead and put your clothes back on. I need to spend this time with Rhonda since Bernard fucked up. Go do some cleaning or something."

Karen quickly got dressed and thanked God as she exited the room.

Rhonda lay back on the bed and relaxed as Nikki licked her lips. *Lance better not fuck this up. This bitch wants to play with me and put the shit in my face like I am suppose to accept it.*

Almost as soon as the thought entered her mind, it was interrupted by a blaring voice on the intercom. "This is the police. We have the house surrounded. Nicole Harris please come out with your hands up."

Nikki sprang from the bed and ran to the window. Rhonda followed behind her. Police were everywhere. She went to where her clothes lay neatly folded and retrieved her gun.

"Oh my goodness." Rhonda responded. "Don't do it Nikki. Give it up. They will kill you. Just go peacefully. I don't want anything to happen to you."

"Are you fucking crazy?" She cried. "I'm not going back to that fuckin looney bin. I can't. I just can't do it. Those people are crazy. Help me. Isn't there another way out of here? A basement or something?"

"Nikki, the house is surrounded. There is no way out. Please don't resist. I don't trust those police. They will kill you."

"Nicole Harris, come out of the house right now with your hands where we can see them." The voice blared again.

"Go ahead Nikki.' Rhonda pleaded. "We'll find a way to get you out but for right now you need to go with them before somebody gets hurt."

Nikki finished dressing. "I'm coming out!" She yelled outside the door. "Don't shoot! I'm coming out." Nikki exclaimed. She slowly opened the door and walked out.

"Show me your hands!" An officer yelled. "NOW!"

Nikki slowly raised her hands and arms above her head. She began to cry. "What did I do? I haven't done anything. Why are y'all pointing those guns at me? I'm getting scared. Don't shoot me. Please don't shoot me. I only stopped by to see my children. What's wrong with that? I didn't do anything. I didn't hurt anybody. Why don't y'all just leave me alone?"

One of the officers placed Nikki's hands behind her back and handcuffed her. "Miss Harris you are under arrest. You have the right to remain silent. If you choose to give up your right to remain silent, anything you say can and will be used against you in a court of law. You have the right to an attorney. If you cannot afford an attorney, one will be appointed to you. Do you understand your rights?"

Nikki looked at the officers as her cries changed to laughter. "I'm not stupid you Moron's. I understand exactly what the hell you are saying. I have the right to be fucked. If I give up the right to be fucked, you will rape me while I am handcuffed and in police custody. I have the right to suck your dick. If I give up that right you will force your dick down my throat and kill me if I bite it. Yes Sir, I understand my rights very well. Let's get this show on the road." She snickered.

The male officers gazed at Nikki as she licked her tongue out and moved her body in a seductive manner.

"Hell to the no!" One of the officers responded.

"No what?" Nikki asked. "You know you want some of this good pussy. Your partner didn't see you wink at me. You are going to take my pussy when you get me away from here aren't you? Where are you going to take me? I know that you are not taking me straight to the station. Are you going to drag me into the woods?" She laughed hysterically. "I'm ready. Which one of you has the biggest dick?"

One of the officers exclaimed, "I'm not putting her in my damn car."

Another officer responded. "Don't worry. A female officer is on the way."

"Damn!" Nikki shook her head. "It would have been fun. I wouldn't have resisted."

A patrol car pulled up with a female officer. After Nikki was put in the car, it sped away. One of the officers looked at the other one. "So you wanted to get some of that huh?" He laughed. "Winking at ol gal."

"Shit! Not on your life man. Do you know who that is? That's Nicole Harris! No way man."

They laughed before getting in their police cars and departing.

Chapter 48

Anthony watched the door half the night. Doctors came in to check on him. Nurses came in to check his vitals. Everybody came except the one person he wanted to see. At half past midnight he finally gave up on seeing Erik. He closed his eyes and wondered why Erik had neither visited or called to check on him.

He couldn't use the excuse that he didn't know because not only had Brandi called him but it was splattered all over the television and radio about the Courthouse shooting. Maybe Brandi was right. He thought as he dozed off to sleep.

"Anthony. Wake up Anthony." Erik whispered.

"I nowed ya wud come."

"I wanted to come earlier but I had an emergency. Besides that, I didn't want anybody to see me. How are you? I've been checking on your condition. It would be inappropriate to say that you dodged a bullet. You were seriously injured man. If it hadn't been for a Higher Power, we wouldn't be having this conversation. You would be dead."

"Man, dat bitch came outta nowhere. I neba seen hur befo. She wuz tryna kill me. Dat bitch wuz really tryna kill me."

"Well she is locked up now so you don't have to worry about that. Listen up. I spoke with Chambers. He feels that there is a possibility you will do a little time but not much. He is trying to work it out with the D.A. that if you take a plea agreement you will serve a maximum of five years. You will in all likelihood be out in about two years. I'm going to look out for you while you are in there"

"What da hell ya mean ya gon look out fer me? I cant do no mo dam time man. Hell nah! I cant do dat shit."

Calm down Anthony. Just calm down. I am going to work things out on my end to make sure your time is as short as possible. There is no getting around you doing some time but I am going to look out for you. You have to trust me on this one." Erik pleaded.

"Hell no. I'm not feelin dat shit one dam bit. Ima be locked up and den wat da hell ya gon be out here doin? Datz sum bullshit man. I can't go bak in dat dam place. Dat wus a hellhole." Anthony raised his voice.

"Shh…hh! Lower your voice Anthony. You are being too loud. I'm telling you that this is the best deal that you are going to get. What else can you do? Oh yeah! You can roll over on me but that won't shorten your time. It will only mean that we will both be doing time and you won't have anyone on the outside to look out for you. Is that what you want Anthony? Do you want me to be locked up with you? Because if that is what you want Anthony, if that is how your love is, I will just go down to the station and turn myself in right now. Just say the word."

Anthony looked at him. "Nah Erik. I don wan ya ta turn yasef in. Dat won help nunthin. It wuz jus hard as hell bein loked up. I thot I'd neba hafta go bak inside agin. I no da two yers will pass by fast but dam. Do ya promise to be der fer me man? Are ya goin to come visit me? You don't eben visit me like dat while I'm out." Anthony's eyes dropped from Erik to the floor.

"Yes Anthony. I will visit you every chance I get. I know that I haven't been here for you like I should have. My foolish pride and worrying about my reputation. It was me being selfish. Please forgive me. I just didn't realize how much you mean to me until you got shot and I stood the chance of losing you. I will visit you every chance I get. You won't have to do this time alone and that is my good word."

"Ok. Tell Mr. Chambers dat he can let da fuckin D.A. know dat Ima take dat plea deal. I'm holdin ya ta ya word Erik. Don let me down." He responded. "Wateba ya do, jus don let me down. I love ya man but I swer on my dead mama dat I will kill ya ass."

"We're straight Anthony. Let me get out of here before the nurse makes her rounds. I will get with Chambers in the morning. Love you." He kissed Anthony on the lip and snuck out of the room as quietly as he had snuck in.

Chapter 49

Karen sprinted from the couch when she heard the sound of a car door closing. Lance walked up the sidewalk looking as though he had lost his best friend. She knew it hadn't been easy for him to give Nikki up but what other choice did he have? He had actually called the police before she gave him the signal. Maybe he was trying to botch things up. Who knows? One thing for sure, it had to end. Nikki couldn't go on dictating their lives indefinitely.

"Hi Lance. Come on in. What's on your mind?" Karen asked him as she stepped aside to allow him entrance.

"A lot Karen. Things happened so fast." He came inside and had a seat. "I know that Nikki was a thorn in both our sides but she did have a good side to her. You know that she could have easily given us up Karen and we'd both be fucked up right now. But she didn't do that."

"I know Lance, and it's not like I don't appreciate it. I never wanted to get involved in her escape in the first place. You are the one who dragged me into this mess. I feel sorry for Nikki but she needs help. She made my life a living hell." Karen sat next to Lance. "Let's just move on and try to get past this. Hopefully Nikki will get the help she needs now. Would you like a drink?"

"Sure. Anything you fix will be fine. Thanks."

"Now what? What happens now Lance? This whole ordeal with Nikki has really changed me. I have to look at myself in the mirror and wonder how I could have been so damn stupid. Oh my goodness!"

Lance took his drink. "Karen you are not a stupid woman. Nikki is very clever. From the moment she was admitted to Brooksville, those wheels started turning in her head. She was determined to get out of there and she didn't care who she used to do it." He looked away.

"Lance, you really did care about her didn't you?" Karen asked.

"I did." He answered. "I loved her. She kept putting me through stuff but I loved her. At one point, I considered leaving my wife for her. She had a way of making me feel good. There was just something special about Nikki. I can't put my finger on it. But there comes a point in a relationship when you realize that a one-sided love affair is the same as no love affair at all."

She felt sorry for Lance. Maybe he could pick up the pieces and get on with his life. He couldn't continue to mope for Nikki. That shit wasn't healthy.

"Karen, I once read something that makes a lot of sense now. I don't know who said it but the advice was basically to examine the people in your life and promote, demote, or terminate. Nikki has been terminated. You have been promoted." He tried to kiss her.

"No Lance." She stopped him. "If by promotion you mean a relationship, the answer is no. I need time to reflect on all that has happened. I'm determined to get my life together. You don't know all of the things that Nikki put me through. Some of those things I would never divulge to anyone. She was hell. And besides that, you have a wife. I'm not being the other woman. I'm not accommodating you in your spare time." She stood. "I think it's time for you to leave."

Lance finished his drink and stood. "I understand. I hope you know it was never my intention to belittle you. We have both been through a lot. You are a remarkable woman. Friends?"

"Always!" She answered.

Lance kissed her on the forehead and walked out the door.

Chapter 50

News of Nikki's capture flooded the airwaves. Bernard raced to the door. Although the locks had not been changed he didn't want Rhonda to feel as if he were intruding. He rang the bell and spoke into the intercom. "It's me Rhonda. May I come in?

"Yes. Come on in Bernard." She answered.

He scurried into the house and found Rhonda sitting at the bar with a drink in front of her. "Are you ok Rhonda? I just heard the news. I came as fast as I could."

"I'm fine Bernard. Nikki has been captured and I'm ready to get on with my life."

"So what about me? What about us Rhonda? Are you still determined to live your life without me? What about the kids?"

Rhonda looked at him with tears in her eyes. Bernard, you don't want me. I wish you did but you don't. You were fucking Nikki long before the rest of this mess started. You had an affair with her and had a baby across town while all the time I thought our marriage was solid."

"I know Baby. I know that I made some terrible mistakes and I was wrong. I'm human Rhonda and I make mistakes. I'm not perfect and I know I hurt you but Baby, I never stopped loving you. Just give me another chance. Please Rhonda. Think about the kids."

She fixed herself another drink. "I've made mistakes also Bernard but you don't realize how badly you have hurt me. That kind of pain doesn't just go away overnight. Each time you fucked Nikki; it tore me to pieces seeing how much you enjoyed having your magic stick all up in her. It chipped away at my heart knowing that my pussy wasn't good enough but there was another woman who you preferred. Knowing I was second best. Oh my goodness Bernard." She cried into her hand.

"That's not true Rhonda. You don't understand and I don't expect you to understand. I do love you. Honestly I do and I never meant to hurt you. Please believe me. It's just that I'm human and I got weak. Nikki knew how to push my buttons. I know that I should have been stronger. Do you know how many times I have wanted to kick my own ass for hurting you? Even now, seeing the pain in your eyes is killing me. You're a good woman Rhonda. I'm so sorry. Please give me a chance to make it up to you."

"Bernard, right now anything that comes out of your mouth is just empty words. I have to have time for me now. I can't keep doing this Nikki shit. And if it's not Nikki, who knows, it may be some other woman. I'm just tired Bernard. I don't want to do this anymore."

"You don't want to do what anymore? You don't want to be married anymore. Please tell me that is not what you are saying?" He joined her at the bar and took her drink out of her hand. "Don't tell me you are thinking about ending our marriage."

She gazed at her husband. It seemed like he had aged over the last week. The once striking, confident and vivacious man was worn. Rhonda felt a slight concern for him, but not enough for her to concede.

"Bernard, right now I don't know what the future holds. It would be unfair for me to say. All I can tell you right now is that we can't live together. We have to remain separated."

"But I don't want a separation." He protested. "Just give me one more chance Rhonda. I'm stronger now. I'm more focused."

"So many times I asked myself why you turned to another woman. What made you step outside the marriage and go far enough to put your magic stick in another woman when it should have been solely for me? An argument? Was that all it took? Couples argue all the time. I was a good wife to you but as I was told a long time ago; men don't appreciate a good woman."

"I do appreciate you Rhonda. I have apologized and told you how sorry I am. There is nothing else I can do. What do I have to do? Do you want me to get on my knees and beg?" He fell down on his knees. "Please forgive me Sweetheart. If you give me another chance, I will spend the rest of my life making this up to you."

"Bernard, I'm sorry." Tears rolled down her face. "I'm not ready for you to try to make it up to me. Dean is old enough to feel the tension. She knows that things are not right. And there's Nard. I need to concentrate on helping him with his social skills and doing whatever I can to ensure he will be the best that he can possibly be. The daycare can't do it all."

As he slowly got up and strolled to the bar to freshen his drink, Bernard asked, "What does the future look like? A separation first and then what? Are you going to start dating someone else? Are we ultimately throwing the towel in and prolonging a divorce? What?"

She laughed. "You sure do have a small mind to be a teacher. Dating is the last thing in the world on my mind. I'm going to concentrate on the kids and on me. You can see them any time you want. It is only right that you be a part of their lives since you were instrumental in getting that bitch pregnant twice." Rhonda looked away. "I'm sorry. I didn't mean to say that."

"Yes you did. You meant to say it. You never pass up an opportunity to throw up in my face, the fact that I got Nikki pregnant while I was married to you." He turned his drink up and swallowed it in a single gulp before walking to the door. "I'm at the Marriott for time being. I'll look for a small apartment next week. Bye Rhonda." He opened the door.

"Wait Bernard." She said.

"Yes?" He asked anxious.

"Your keys." Rhonda held out her hand. He took the house keys off his key ring and placed them in her hand.

"I love you Rhonda. No matter what you believe, I do love you." He kissed her on the cheek before closing the door.

Rhonda stood with her back against the door and began to cry. "I love you too." She whispered.

The telephone rang. She walked over to the table and checked the caller ID before answering. "Hi Brandi. What's up? Yeah, I heard about Anthony taking the plea agreement. Are you ok? I know. Me neither. What do you say about two broken hearts getting away this weekend to visit Shemeka? Great. I will make arrangements for the kids. Time for a new beginning." She hung up the telephone.

Printed in the United States
By Bookmasters